ALSO BY MAX ALLAN COLLINS

———

COME SPY WITH ME

John Sand Book One

MAX ALLAN COLLINS

WITH

MATTHEW V. CLEMENS

WOLFPACK
PUBLISHING
— EST 2013 —

WOLFPACK
PUBLISHING
— EST 2013 —

Come Spy With Me

Paperback Edition
Copyright © 2020 Max Allan Collins

Wolfpack Publishing
6032 Wheat Penny Avenue
Las Vegas, NV 89122

wolfpackpublishing.com

Paperback ISBN: 978-1-64734-533-4
eBook ISBN: 978-1-64734-205-0
Library of Congress Control Number: 2020948751

COME SPY WITH ME

In memory of
ENNIS WILLIE
The original Sand man

"All history is love and violence."
Ian Fleming

ONE

HOLIDAY ROYALE
JUNE 1960

CHAPTER ONE
BEACHFRONT SAND

The slim shapely blonde at the front desk, her Caribbean-colorful blouse offering just the right touch of cleavage, regarded the man before her with obvious interest.

"Name?"

Somehow she had managed to make out of that one word several promising syllables.

The tall tan dark-haired guest *Life* magazine had once described as "cruelly handsome" rewarded her interest with a flicker of a grin; though his athletic build was somewhat concealed by casual vacation attire—pastel blue sport jacket, yellow Ban-Lon sports shirt, white khaki slacks—the pretty young clerk's response was not, in his experience, unusual.

In fact, there had been a time—not all that long ago—when he'd have taken the fine young woman's flirtation as a gauntlet thrown down that he'd have gladly snatched up, a challenge routinely met though anything but routinely executed.

Not now.

Those recent days were already in the distant past.

All he gave the hotel employee, in his vaguely aristocratic British baritone, was an indifferent, "Sand. John Sand."

Amusement touched the corners of the desk clerk's full lips. "You have a reservation, Mr. Sand?"

"I do."

Her tone was flippant as she flipped through her card file. "That rather sounds like a marriage vow."

"If you check my booking," he said, twitching another smile, "you'll find you're not far wrong. I've secured the honeymoon suite."

"You have indeed," the desk clerk said, but her tone conveyed no enthusiasm; she was all business suddenly. "Ah, here it is." She withdrew a card. "But where is Mrs. Sand?"

"Doing her wifely duties."

Amusement again. "Putting her to work already, Mr. Sand?"

"No. She's off spending money."

"Oh dear."

"It's all right. It's hers." He half-turned and nodded across the lobby toward the gift shop where Stacey, his bride of barely twenty-four hours, was examining Jamaican trinkets as if they were evidence at a crime scene.

"Why, she's *lovely*," the desk clerk said, and it was almost a gasp.

Sand arched an eyebrow at the young woman, as if to say, *Would you have expected less of me?*

Five foot four, her auburn hair rolling in waves to her mid-spine, the former Stacey Boldt's eight-stone weight had been perfectly arranged by her own efforts and that of a helpful God. That same *Life* writer had said of her that she might have been the long lost sister of the woman many Americans hoped would be their next First Lady.

No pink pillbox hats for Stacey, however—far too tame, nor would she likely follow any other female's fashion lead. If the two women had indeed been siblings, Sand's choice of sisters was clearly the one born in the wild. Jackie Bouvier would almost certainly be too sophisticated, too pristine, to go scuba diving among the underwater ruins of a sunken city.

For Sand's choice of a bride, however, such an adventure seemed the perfect honeymoon activity.

Well, one of them.

And now here they were, checking into the opulent Mayfair Hotel overlooking Kingston Harbour.

"Stunning as she is, Mr. Sand," the young woman brazenly said, as he signed the register, "I'm somewhat surprised John Sand would settle for one woman."

At one time, being recognized as a sort of celebrity by fetching females like this one had been a boon; now it seemed a burden, if not as bad as the men who wanted to buy him a drink and hear stories.

"You might be surprised, Madeline..." That was how her name plate identified her. "...by how mundane much of my life has been. Don't be deceived by what you read in the paperbacks, or the tabloid press."

"I trust your honeymoon will be anything but 'mundane,' Mr. Sand," the desk clerk said, licking her lips perhaps to impart a touch of glistening missed opportunity. "And I do hope you and Mrs. Sand will have a memorable stay with us."

Such encounters with strangers, including even this comely clerk, had become common occurrences in the life of John Sand, and represented one of the primary reasons for his early retirement from MI6, the United Kingdom's Secret Intelligence Service.

Ever since a longtime friend and former colleague of his had begun writing those thinly veiled and somewhat ridiculously exaggerated novels based on Sand's assignments, the undercover intelligence operative had been unable to perform his duties with any sort of anonymity. A secret agent, after all, must remain, well—secret.

And Sand's secret was out.

First it had been Sunday supplement fluff pieces. And then that *Life* magazine article and photo spread labeled Sand the "real" hero of JFK's favorite espionage novels, leading to more such unwanted publicity, until his effectiveness as a cloak-and-dagger man was now nil. Particularly since the books had started hitting the bestseller lists, and Hollywood (his former colleague had told him with embarrassed pleasure) had come knocking.

A hand touched his back and Sand turned to find Stacey facing him, her chin tilted, a small brown bag clutched in her other hand.

"Find something that appeals, love?" he asked her, nodding toward the gift shop.

Stacey's puffy Bardot-ish lips formed the familiar smile that seemed half pout, half promise, while her green eyes took in the pretty receptionist.

"Why," she said, "have you?"

Stacey's faint but distinct Texas accent bumped up incongruously against his cultured British tones.

The desk clerk, far more matter-of-fact now that Stacey was on the other side of the counter too, handed Sand a pair of keys. "Room 721, Mr. Sand."

Sand nodded.

"I'll have your bags sent up immediately....I hope you and Mrs. Sand will have a wonderful stay here at the Mayfair. Enjoy Port Royal."

He gave the woman a quick smile and a nod, and then he and his wife were walking to the elevators. On the way, he gestured to the tiny brown bag clutched in his bride's left hand. "Something for me?"

Her contagious laugh bubbled up, then receded like a wave. "In a way."

Sand arched an eyebrow.

"New earrings," she explained, hefting the tiny bag.

"I'm quite sure I'll look simply smashing in them."

Her laugh returned. "I would *pay* to see that, darlin'."

"Oh, there'll be no charge."

In their suite, Stacey disappeared into the bath, leaving Sand with the black bellman. After depositing their suitcases in the bedroom, the stocky bellman, perhaps thirty-five, discreetly accepted the five-pound note Sand slipped into his hand without meeting Sand's eyes.

"Sir," Sand said.

The bellman looked up, startled. "Yes, Mr. Sand?"

Their eyes met.

"Should I need further help, might I have your name?"

"Luis."

The two men nodded at each other and exchanged the faintest smiles.

Closing the door behind the bellman, Sand reflected. Though native-born blacks made up a staggering majority of the population here, they held down mostly menial jobs such as bellman or busboy at the hotel. Sand knew that one day the price for such inequities on this island would have to be paid. Apparently India hadn't taught his countrymen much of anything.

Sand had his first good look at the sitting room. Not long ago, his next act would have been to thoroughly search the entire suite for bugging devices. But that was the past with all its trials and dangers—and this was the pleasant present of his honeymoon.

With its wallpaper of white flowers on a sea green background, the sitting room had the feel of a garden. A wide white sofa occupied one wall, a low mahogany coffee table in front of it. At angles facing the sofa were wing chairs covered in a light green brocade that matched the walls. A television on a stand had been provided for fools with nothing better to do.

Sand ambled past the small wet bar to the French doors that opened onto a balcony overlooking Kingston Harbour.

Bright sunshine kissed the cool blue bay, reflecting in shimmering white off the gentle wave tips that meandered to the alabaster beach on the soft breeze. Across busy Kingston Harbour, barely visible in the afternoon glare, lay Port Royal, once considered the wickedest place in the known world, two-thirds of it now beneath the sea. Tomorrow, they would hire a small boat and he and Stacey would dive on the ruins of a once mighty town that had been swept away in the earthquake of 1692.

Behind him, Sand heard the bathroom door open.

Though retirement had been forced upon him by his colleague's novels—as well as the fact that Sand's body carried more lead in it than a crate of number two pencils—he relished his new freedom and the time it would allow him to spend with Stacey, who was as rich as she was beautiful.

She asked casually, "How do you like my new earrings?"

He turned to face her and his breath caught. In tah-dah fashion, she stood before him, half a room away, two long jade cats dangling from her ears.

She wore nothing else.

With an appreciative smile, he took in her deeply tanned curves with their echoes of bikini in the minimum of white flesh untouched by sun. The firm, full, perfectly shaped breasts, tip-tilted with youth's defiance of gravity, the sweet puffy pinkness of her nipples with their generous aureoles daring him to do something about them, the smooth supple belly with its tiny navel that winked at him when she laughed, the strong thighs, well-turned calves, the tangled tuft of her pubic triangle...all of it his. This woman, to whom nakedness with the lights on was no challenge at all, was adjusting the earrings with not a trace of nervousness or self-consciousness in her demeanor.

Crossing slowly to him, jade cats dangling from her lobes, she drawled, "What's wrong with the pride of MI6? Cat got your tongue?"

"Not yet it hasn't."

They embraced. She was strong for her size, her arms draping around his neck and drawing his face to hers, her lips finding his with a hunger he matched. They kissed for a very long time, softly at first, then with increasing passion as their urgency rose.

Breaking away, with an erection his divining rod, Sand made his way to the bedroom door as she tagged after him like a friendly kitten.

He turned to walk backward and commented, finally, blandly, "I approve."

"Of what?"

"The earrings."

"Is that all you have to say?"

"Such a pretty pair of pussies," he said, and tapped one of the earrings and made it swing a little. Then he disappeared into the bedroom, barely murmuring, "Or should I say trio?...Here kitty kitty...."

She trotted in after him, and quickly stripped him of his jacket, shoulder holster, and shirt, unzipping this, tugging that, tossing items as if emptying a drawer in a hurry; then she trailed her fingers over the black curls on his chest, traced rippling muscles, the scars of bullets and blades recording a chequered history. Gently, she began kissing each scar.

It took a while.

Her lips against his chest, her words were muffled: "Why do you insist on still carrying that awful thing?"

"If it's so awful why do you have hold of it?"

"No, silly. That *weapon.* That ugly gun."

"Ah."

"You're retired, John, you're on your honeymoon—and you should start *acting* like it."

"Excellent suggestion," he said, sweeping her into his arms and dropping her onto the bed like an ice cube into a drink. "*Right now....*"

For the next hour, only moans and gasps punctuated the silence of the suite, those and the faint laughs and squeals of vacationers on the beach beyond their windows.

When they were sweaty and satisfied, he grinned at her. "I hope once is enough for now."

Stacey peered down over the slopes of her breasts at him, quizzically. "Nothing here to perk your interest again?"

"I am not a young man anymore, my love."

And he wasn't. Even though he was only thirty-six to her twenty-eight, he had crammed a great deal of living and trying not to die into the last twenty, beginning with his role in the Home Guard during the London Blitz at sixteen and continuing through a lifetime's worth of cheating disaster in settings from posh to sordid and every stop between, all over the world.

"Time you were put out to pasture, you think?" she asked, as they both sat up, her finger playing lightly across his leg. As her hand moved lazily, Stacey leaned closer, lips brushing his ear, his chest, then his stomach. "Or maybe you'd prefer...out to stud?"

Sand tried to speak but no words found their way out as Stacey's kisses moved down him, pushing him almost roughly back against the bed. He managed only a slight moan as she returned the favors he had so recently done her.

The two of them achieved release simultaneously, the woman riding the man this time, their world reduced only to the space they occupied as wave upon wave crashed over them, even as waves crashed on the beach out their open window, with tourist laughter and squeals echoing.

Finally Stacey rolled off him.

The warm Jamaican breeze wafted through the window, sheer curtains whispering even as the honeymooners whispered their love. They kissed tenderly, passion spent but love unceasing, kissing like young sweethearts, reminding Sand of that very first time with her, back in a guest room at her father's ranch near Houston.

Sand had been sent to investigate Stacey's father, Noah "Dutch" Boldt, who was suspected by MI6 and the CIA of trying to corner the world oil market through contrived terrorist activities. Posing as a business rival's second-in-command, offering to betray his boss, Sand infiltrated Boldt's inner circle, where he met Stacey. The chemistry had been instant, sexual sparks igniting deeper feelings.

And when, over the course of their heated affair, Stacey learned Sand's true identity, she responded without anger, helping him to understand that her oil tycoon father was not the criminal mastermind the spy's superiors envisaged. Rather, Dutch Boldt was actively attempting to derail the megalomaniacal machinations of his longtime business partner, the out-of-control Jake Lonestarr. Enraged when Boldt wouldn't go along with his self-serving scenario, the lunatic Lonestarr kidnaped his partner's daughter and held her hostage aboard his yacht, the *Cuba Libre.*

One moonless midnight in the Gulf of Mexico, with Dutch Boldt at his side in a small launch, Sand slipped up alongside the sleeping yacht and boarded it in darkness, when every light in the world came on and revealed Lonestarr waiting, the tall cadaverous Texan backed by his hulking in-house assassin, Raven, an American Indian with a sadistic streak.

Following Sand onto the deck, Boldt was greeted by a fatal fusillade of automatic gunfire courtesy of his former partner. Diving for cover, Sand responded by punching two rounds from his Walther P38 into the crackpot's chest, sending the Texan tumbling over the rail into the Gulf.

Howling like a wounded beast, Raven hurtled himself at Sand, taking the agent down and pummeling him mercilessly with massive rock-hard fists. Sand's right hand fumbled onto a gaffer's hook and raked the Indian across the face, incurring another yowling scream, then slammed him alongside the head with the thing, leaving the assassin unconscious and bleeding, probably dying.

Then Sand moved through the ship, searching for Stacey, dispatching gun-wielding crew members as he went, the smell of cordite scorching the sea air.

Finding the girl drugged but alive, he scuttled the *Cuba Libre,* escaping in the motorized launch with a groggy Stacey in his arms and her father's body at their feet, a madman's dreams burning orange in the night.

Now, many months later, Sand lay watching Stacey sleeping, her head resting on his shoulder, her full, sensual lips pursed slightly, her body warm against him, stirring something deep within him, only some of it physical. Slowly, as if anticipating his need, she opened her eyes.

"As I was saying," he said, "before you interrupted me...those are splendid earrings."

She laughed deep in her throat. "They're about the only things of mine you kept your hands off. I was afraid you didn't like them."

"They are...how shall I put it? The cat's meow."

Groaning, Stacey pulled away from him and slapped him playfully across the chest. "You are *shameless*."

"Let me show you how much so," he said, once again taking her into his arms.

And the demonstration of his lack of shame that followed took all of ninety seconds, more or less—but in that minute and a half, much was accomplished.

Gasping for breath, she leaned back on her elbows, the fine smooth planes of her body beaded with sweat, saying, "Short but sweet...."

He arched an eyebrow. "Short?"

"Well...in reference to duration only. You have... *remarkable* recuperative powers. For a man who isn't young anymore."

"For an old retired workhorse, you mean?"

"Yes," she said, "for an old retired workhorse," and she sprang from the bed and ran bare-ass to the bathroom, where he soon heard the shower.

Thinking of her in there, naked in her steamy cubicle, soaping herself under those needles of water, Sand considered going in and showing her just how remarkable his recuperative powers really were. He might be old at thirty-six, but...he *was* still only thirty-six....

Then he shrugged, and said to himself, "No need to be a showoff...or a glutton, either," and went looking for his *Gauloises* cigarettes.

An hour later they sat for a dinner in the hotel's lavish restaurant, a pleasingly tacky display dominated by pastels and seashells. The tuxedo fit Sand like it had been tailored for him on Saville Row, which it had—posh attire that reminded him of elegant if dangerous days when *chemin de fer* and other games were played for far greater stakes than mere money.

Not that tonight wasn't elegant in its own right, if dangerous no longer, which was fine by him.

Across the table, Stacey's strapless blue gown showed enough of her ample cleavage to draw glances from male diners at nearby tables. With her sun-highlighted dark hair piled on top of her head, the effect accentuated her graceful, elongated neck. He knew, with a certain pride and even arrogance, which he hoped was at least restrained, that he and his new bride were handsome young animals worth every bit of the envy of others.

Sand smiled approvingly at his wife. "You're being stared at," he said, careful to keep his voice low.

Returning the smile with just a hint of even, white teeth in their bright red frame, she said, "How do you know they're not staring at you?"

"Because," he said, lighting up a cigarette with a match, "they are not women."

"Hah. But the women are looking, too, which you would know if your investigative skills hadn't lost their finely honed edge."

"Looking at me?"

"Hard to say. I might be the object. They may be drawn to that certain glow only a bride can achieve. Or maybe they're sizing up the competition."

"Should either of us be jealous, do you think?"

She shook her head. "Let them dream. Both sexes. We have each other."

"We do at that." He raised his water glass in a toast.

She did the same, but then something behind him caught her eyes, which widened in...fear?

Spinning in his chair, Sand quickly scanned the room...

...but saw nothing, other than the door to the kitchen, swinging back and forth.

His eyes returned to her. Stacey's hand had gone to her mouth and the color had drained from her face.

"What is it?" he asked.

"I could've sworn..."

He was on his feet, coming around the table to her, then lowered himself to put an arm around her. "Stacey, darling—what *is* it?"

The maître d'—a thin, shiny-headed man of perhaps fifty—approached their table with practiced concern. "Is everything all right, madam? Sir?"

Sand nodded automatically, his eyes still on Stacey.

"I'm fine," she said more to the maître d' than to Sand. "I was feeling just a bit faint for a moment."

The maître d' paused, then smiled, nodded and made his careful way back to his station. As Stacey sipped from her water glass, Sand resumed his seat.

He said, "You looked as if someone just walked over your grave."

She shivered, then nodded. "More like I walked over someone *else's* grave."

"What do you mean?"

"I...I could swear I saw a dead man walk across this room."

He sat forward. "Who?"

Stacey was shaking her head. "Not someone easy to mistake, either."

"*Who?*"

"...Raven."

"What? Not possible."

"I know. I saw you sink the *Cuba Libre* with him still on board. I saw the blood. I saw the flames."

Nodding, Sand said, "As did I."

But suddenly he doubted himself. Too often a resilient adversary had turned back up again, with a grudge that had festered into obsession.

As they finished their dinner quietly, exchanging occasional smiles and comments, something dark had dulled the celebratory mood. For the first time in this new marriage he felt a certain irritation—with his young bride, yes, but as much at himself as her.

He feared he should never have followed her advice and left his shoulder-holstered Walther P38 in their room.

CHAPTER TWO
HARBOUR FRIGHTS

———

Could that bastard Raven have survived somehow?

After all, rats had been known to abandon a sinking ship.

Sand would take nothing for granted, certainly not when the woman he loved was at his side. His writer friend had asked permission, in a forthcoming novel, to kill off a character loosely based upon the ex-agent's new wife, and that had been fine with Sand. The sooner fiction could depart from the reality of his life the better.

But he was not about to let a fictional tragedy become a real one.

After a good night's sleep, and a fine morning romp, the couple rented a boat to take them out over the Port Royal ruins. Fracas, the vessel's Jamaican skipper—tall, broad-shouldered, with espresso-colored skin and close-cropped ebony hair—had worked with Sand on more than one occasion, including the *Señor Sí* affair.

After the possible Raven sighting in the hotel restaurant last night, the former intelligence agent was doing his best to conceal from his bride how on edge he felt. Enlisting as their boat captain a frequent MI6 asset only seemed prudent, particularly since Stacey didn't know who—or what—Fracas was. No need to alarm her.

Ruining a honeymoon was no way to start a marriage.

By the time the boat anchored over the sunken city, Stacey seemed to have consigned last night's unpleasant moment to some distant place in her mind. Either that or she was an even better actor than Sand himself, who right now was thinking only of the woman's beauty as he watched her slipping the straps of the scuba tank over her shoulders.

Her one-piece white bathing suit hid few secrets, flattening out her full breasts in a fetching manner, plumping them above the cut of the cloth's neckline. Fracas noticed her allure himself, judging by the way the Jamaican kept himself busy with work around the tiny boat that kept him close to the beautiful young woman.

Sand couldn't blame Fracas for wanting to stay near such a living Venus, particularly one with arms. He couldn't think of anywhere in the world he'd rather be than next to this goddess—so tanned and lithely curvaceous, her dark auburn hair hanging loosely down her back.

As for Fracas, Sand's old comrade may have been less intoxicated by Stacey's charms and more sobered as to the dangers she faced, Sand having shared with his old crony his husbandly concerns about last night's possible sighting.

"Aren't you ready yet?" Stacey asked him. "And why are you grinning like the cat that ate the canary?"

He almost said, *More like the canary that ate the pussy.* But such remarks were best reserved for the boudoir.

So Sand said instead, "Just enjoying the pleasant company."

Fracas grinned. "Thank you, boss."

Sand said to Stacey, "Be ready in a moment, m'love."

Hefting his own tank, he slung it over his shoulders,

snapped the strap across his chest, slipped on his flippers, and followed Stacey over the side in a splash into what might have been a warm, welcoming bath.

Treading water, Sand filled the mask with seawater, dumped it out, then snugged it down over his face. Stacey, treading, did the same and gave him a thumbs up. He returned the gesture as she disappeared into the lapping waves of silty green. He adjusted his mouthpiece, then somersaulted to follow his wife down.

They had been under for nearly half an hour when Sand lost sight of Stacey as she swam off to investigate a huge section of a brick wall that seemed to have sunk mostly intact. He trailed her by maybe three hundred yards as he glided and kicked toward where he'd seen her rounding a corner of that sunken wall.

At its crumbling brick corner, Sand glanced down at the seabed and saw the small cloth bag Stacey had been using to collect relics. His heart leaped into his throat.

There seemed to be a shadow of red in the murky water!

Looking around wildly, Sand scoured the area for any other sign of her. Carefully examining the area near the wall, Sand finally picked up an old brick and noticed a smudge of blood along one edge. Struggling to control his breathing, he swam in ever widening circles around the fallen wall.

On his fourth circuit, Sand caught a glimpse of a diver's fins kicking away from him perhaps twenty feet above and ten to his right. Swimming after his target, Sand cut through water like a knife in an effort to catch the fleeing swimmer, whose identity was lost in the churned blur— *could it be Stacey?* As he closed in from beneath his target, he realized the answer was no.

This was a man, and not just any man—muscular, a head

taller than his pursuer, but just as black-haired, in white trunks emphasizing the reddish-brown cast of his flesh.

Raven!

Adrenaline surged through Sand as he ascended, catching the bastard around the waist just as they broke the surface. The swimmer spit out his mouthpiece and howled in surprise as MI6's most notorious assassin wrenched his captive out of the water, the man gurgling as Sand rolled him over and shoved him splashing down beneath the surface.

Stacey might be gone, but Sand would exact his revenge right here, right now....

Even as the diver struggled, Sand—his rage ice cold despite warm tropical waters lapping around him—could feel the man's strength starting to ebb.

"*John!*"

Stacey's voice!

Behind him, echoing across the water....

"John, what in the name of God are you *doing?*"

Easing but not releasing his grip, treading water, Sand looked up to see Stacey and Fracas standing on the deck of the boat a mere twenty feet away. Stacey's face was twisted in horror, as the Jamaican paused agape as in the midst wrapping Mrs. Sand's left forearm in gauze.

Sand looked at the half-drowned man in his grip and encountered the gagging, terrified countenance of someone he had never seen before.

Relaxing his hold on the stranger, trying to replace harm with help, Sand was rebuffed as the swimmer slapped at the water, backing off from this attacker turned Samaritan, stroking frantically if unsteadily toward Fracas's boat. The Jamaican helped the man aboard while a mortified Sand was left to climb over the side on his own, dripping water and embarrassment.

"I thought..." Sand began, breathing hard, yet even as he caught his breath no more words would come out.

Stacey clearly understood at once what he'd put himself through.

"I cut my arm on that brick wall," she explained. "I looked all over for you, but I thought I'd better get to the surface so Fracas could patch me up before I attracted any sharks."

She showed him her half-bandaged arm, displaying it like evidence before the bench.

But it would take more than that to convince South Dakota businessman Leon Whitefield not to press attempted murder charges against John Sand. Had it been left solely up to Sand's brand of diplomacy, the ex-agent might have been headed for a cell in the Kingston jail.

But ultimately the sincerity of a beautiful woman in a snug white bathing suit, with a smile and a hint of Texas accent, had served well in cooling this gentleman off.

"What would you say, Mr. Whitefield," Stacey said in conclusion, "to letting a nervous honeymooning couple pay for the rental of your diving equipment?"

The businessman was weakening.

Sand said, "And stake you to a nice dinner, perhaps? Janga soup? Curried lobster?"

That did the trick.

When their unexpected guest departed into the waters, Sand said, "Reasonable fella."

"Yes, isn't he?" Stacey said.

"You folks too generous," Fracas said. "I mean, boss, you only *almost* killed him."

***

As night settled in, the lights of the city did their best to compete with a sky flung carelessly with stars, as Sand walked along the harbour with Stacey's arm looped in his.

He probably should have felt at peace here in a tropical paradise, however tainted by tourism, since for once he was not tasked with investigating or assassinating someone for MI6. Instead he was strolling along with a stunningly beautiful, impossibly wealthy bride on his arm, and for the first time since he'd been recruited into the intelligence service, he could walk the streets unarmed...and feel reasonably secure about it.

And yet, in his custom Saville Row tux, he felt naked, jaybird naked.

Well, that was an exaggeration—but certainly the garment didn't fit as it should, having been tailored to accommodate the shoulder-holstered Walther P38. At dinner last night, he'd experienced the jacket's same loose, uncomfortable sensation, and promised himself he wouldn't go out again without the weapon tucked under his left arm, a properly well-dressed *former* secret agent about town.

Particularly after that sighting of a man who might have been Raven.

But in the light of day, after that unfortunate, embarrassing Whitefield incident, Sand feared he was ushering in paranoia, making himself imagine all sorts of non-existent perils. He was retired, after all. An "old" married man now.

Stacey's yellow gown had only the tiniest spaghetti straps holding it in place, her bosom seemingly trying to make a break for it; the sheer canary shawl over her shoulders warded off the slight evening chill, her small matching purse providing just enough room for a lipstick, a compact, and a modest comb. She wore the gauze bandage on her forearm with the pride of a battle survived.

"Quite a performance from my man today," she said without looking at him.

Next to them, the harbour waters lapped against the squat brick wall bordering the cement walkway; they might have been walking alongside a vast swimming pool.

"Made a fool of myself," he said, matter of fact.

"A lovely fool. The kind of fool any woman would want defending her."

"It's just that I thought I'd lost you, and...well."

She squeezed his arm a little tighter. "Your heart is definitely in the right place, John. But please tell me you won't be making a habit of attacking strangers, now, won't you, darlin'?"

Sand forced a grin. "Not a *habit*, love. A practice perhaps, if I feel you're threatened."

Just ahead, swerving through the darkness, some poor inebriated soul in an oversize, lightweight raincoat tottered toward a backless bench, one of the many lining the harbour every fifteen yards or so. Seeing the figure ease down and sit, Sand moved closer to Stacey, the couple nearer the water's edge now, as they strolled along the narrow sidewalk.

She said, a bit teasingly, "You still seem tense, my dear. Perhaps I should take you back to the hotel where I can assist you in...*relievin'* your tension. Aid you in easing away some of that excess energy."

He had a remark ready, but motion to the left caused his eyes to move from his wife to the boozer on the bench, who was trying to stagger to his feet.

Then, as if someone had thrown a switch, the figure reached out and snatched Stacey and flung her like a rag doll against the bench, which struck her in the back and sent her sliding down to lay sprawled, half on the grass, half on the pavement, motionless.

Sand could not run to her, blocked by that seeming souse who now stood tall, filling out the droopy raincoat, a stooped Dr. Jekyll now a tall Mr. Hyde. A jagged scar ran from the corner of his right eye to his jawline like a luminous pink worm, a disfigurement glistening in the moonlight against the dark, coldly crazed face.

No false alarm this time, but confirmation of what they had indeed seen the night before.

"Raven," Sand growled, dropping into a hunched, high-fisted combat stance.

The Indian held his ground, a nine-millimeter pistol in his right hand. "I brought wedding presents," he said, in the low rumble that passed for his voice.

Then with his free hand, which was no larger than a catcher's mitt, the Indian withdrew something from a deep side pocket of the large, loose coat: *a gaffer's hook.* On its short, sawed-off pole, the curved steel glinted in the moonlight.

"This is for your new wife," Raven said. "She will live, but every morning her mirror will remind her of what *you* did to *me.*"

The big man touched the hook to his face as if the scar needed any help in making his point.

"And this," Raven said, extending his arm and aiming the gun at Sand's belly, where a bullet wound would take its own sweet time killing him, "is for *you....*"

Sand pitched sideways, off the walkway and over its short drop-off into the harbour, disappearing down into the deep water, its warmth gone, replaced by evening chill, as Raven got off one wild shot that made unlikely thunder under so clear a night sky.

***

Stacey came around to see the imposing figure–*Raven!*–looking into the swirling waters of the harbour, gripping a gun in one hand and a hooked instrument in the other. Then he turned his attention to her as she clambered to her feet, her shawl gone, the small purse lost in the scuffle.

"What kind of 'bounder' runs out on a woman on their honeymoon?" the Indian asked her rhetorically, a tight smile cutting through the scar dividing his face into ugly halves. As he bore down on her, her eyes searched the night for an escape route or some beachfront rambler who might help.

No route.

No help.

But she would not run—she had been trained to defend herself, and now she was the one who lowered into a combat stance.

That only amused Raven, who swished that hook back and forth, the metal whistling nastily through the air. A lion playing with its prey, he snarled, "You'll still have that nice body...I'm not greedy...I just want to get *even*—"

A figure exploded from the water behind the Indian, a figure with a rock almost too big for a fist to grip it; but a fist *was* gripping it, *Sand* was gripping it, the crudest of basic weapons salvaged from the bottom of the nearby water. The splash of Sand surfacing made Raven spin and he had time to raise and aim the pistol and fire...

...but not enough time to stop the dripping man in the tuxedo, who had popped up like a posh jack-in-the box to hurl that stone.

The thunderous gunshot and the thick crack of the stone slamming into the Indian's frontal bone reverberated off the water and into the night, the second sound like an echo of the first.

The Indian staggered in a parody of ancient campfire dances, then dropped both the gun and the hook as he slumped to the sidewalk, onto his knees, as if praying to some god or other. Then he flopped onto his face.

Stacey had sucked in a breath the moment her husband rose from the water and now she finally let it out, as Sand again slipped below the surface, an apparition that had come and gone.

She picked up the pistol and, as she moved past the fallen Raven, kept the weapon trained on her attacker. Then she moved to the harbour wall's edge, her eyes scouring the surface for her husband.

"Where are you?" she muttered. "Where in God's name *are* you, John...?"

At last, a hand extended from the drink and, like a man in the dark searching for the light switch, Sand grasped at the edge of the wall bordering the walk. "If...if you please...."

The unconscious Raven forgotten, Stacey helped Sand pull himself out of the water, his left arm dangling uselessly; he flopped onto the cement walkway like a big fish onto a boat deck.

"He *shot* you," she said, aghast.

His sopping tux as slick and black as a seal, Sand shrugged one shoulder. "So it would seem."

"What happened to that gun of yours?"

"Someone told me not to carry it."

She frowned and scolded, "What kind of marriage are we going to have if you listen to everything I say?"

Sand grinned. "An eventful one, it would seem."

"You're only to listen to me," she said, "when I'm right," and she hugged his wet carcass to her.

Sand was about to kiss her when something else—someone else—caught his attention. Her eyes went where her husband's did.

Raven was on his feet and in motion.

That gaffer's hook was in his massive hand again, as the brute dove toward the couple who were still locked in an embrace. Sand grabbed the pistol from his wife's hand and—as the Indian raised the hook, ready to swing it—fired once. And twice.

The first bullet caught Raven in the chest, getting his attention, standing him up straight.

The second entered through his left eye, exiting in a spray of bone and blood and brain, a gaudy holiday streamer, and the Indian slumped into a heap at their feet, in final surrender.

"Nevermore," Sand said.

***

Morning sunshine arrived before they began their weary walk from the constable's station back to their hotel. The police had grilled the honeymooners thoroughly, even while Sand's shoulder was being patched up by a doctor from the British governor's office. The bullet had gone through clean, missing arteries, and would amount to nothing more than yet another scar. Sand requested a phone call, which he made to the Home Secretary in London, who called the governor, who phoned the police chief, and the couple was, finally, released.

As they walked to the hotel, Sand's face remained a mask of barely concealed anger.

"Don't be a spoilsport," Stacey said as they neared the hotel. "It's over. We've won—we're safe again."

"Do you really think our post-wedding well-wisher showed up of his own accord?"

Stacey frowned. "What else could have brought him?"

"*Who* else, you mean."

"Why, do you think he's serving a new master?"

"Possibly," he said. "But what if his longtime employer is still out there?"

Her eyes showed white all around. "Jake Lonestarr?"

Sand shrugged, perhaps trying to minimize the possibility for her sake. "If Raven survived...perhaps his boss did, too."

"John—what does that mean to us? Dutch Boldt's daughter and her new husband?"

He took in a breath and let it out. "It means, my dear, that until I can ascertain whether Jake Lonestarr is indeed as dead as a barbecued steer, we may have other unpleasant surprises in our future together. And one other thing."

"Yes?"

"Perhaps I'm not as retired as we'd hoped."

Later, at the hotel, as they entered their room, she said, "Maybe you *should* wear that gun."

He laughed. "I admit I didn't understand your attitude in that regard. After all, you Texans are usually fairly keen on keeping your shooting irons handy. Shall I put mine on now, after I get out of this poor soggy tux? It is almost time for breakfast."

Wrapping her arms around him gently to baby his wounded arm, and hers, she said, "No, darlin'. I've got other plans for us."

"Such as what?"

"Such as breakfast in bed."

She dropped the straps off her shoulders, allowing the gown to pool at her feet, and stood naked before him.

"We had that yesterday," he said.

She returned the smile and said, "Married men have to get used to leftovers."

TWO

FROM CUBA,
YOURS CORDIALLY

MAY 1961

CHAPTER THREE
DOMINICAN DOMINOES

His sleeves rolled up, his suit jacket tossed carelessly on the passenger seat of his rented car, John Sand closed his eyes and thought of England.

This brought a glimmer of a smile, but did nothing at all to dissipate the intense Dominican heat. His tie, its Windsor knot loosened at the neck, hung limply against his damp white shirt.

Accelerating firmly, Sand urged the '56 Chevy convertible on, the vehicle vibrating like a Waring blender as it knocked along hitting on six of its eight cylinders. The fractional addition of speed managed to barely increase the breeze coming over the windscreen, a mostly fruitless gesture only serving to swirl the hot air around more.

Sand's meeting with General Rafael Trujillo replayed in his mind as he drove down a two-lane blacktop that the Dominican government insisted was a major highway. The former intelligence agent had come to this hothouse climate in his relatively new role as the executive vice president of Boldt Oil.

He had hoped to return to Houston with a signed contract allowing Boldt to begin test drilling in a clearing that company scouts had picked out in the jungle outside Ciudad Trujillo. Formerly known as Santo Domingo, the capital had been re-christened by General Trujillo, thus allowing the citizens of the Dominican Republic to honor him and his family.

Lucky them, Sand thought.

A barrel-chested man who perpetually hid behind dark glasses, General Trujillo kept Sand waiting for over an hour in this broiling heat before finally appearing at the proposed drilling site in an air-conditioned black limousine. Naturally, Sand's car had no such extravagance and he had spent the time slow cooking in his own juices, like the other meats in the *Sancocho de Siete Carnes* he'd been served at his hotel yesterday evening.

The caws of jungle birds seemed oddly skeptical, but Sand remained hopeful. Both parties stood to make out in this deal. That the negotiation would take place along a narrow access road in the midst of a humid, fetid jungle added a strange ambience; but business was business, no matter where it was conducted.

"*Mi amigo,*" the General said as he stepped from the back door of the limo.

For the briefest of moments Sand felt the exhilarating rush of cool air from the limousine before the chauffeur closed the door, and sealed it away.

Sand nodded respectfully. "General Trujillo."

The General gestured rather grandly. "I am sorry to have kept you waiting, Señor Sand, but—as I am sure you understand—the affairs of state do make their demands."

Sand said, "Of course, General," and offered his hand.

The General, in his garishly decorated dress uniform, might have been a doorman at the Savoy; but this was the leader of a Caribbean country, who clasped the other's hand then let it go, as if at this stage holding on longer would be too much of a commitment.

With no further preamble, Trujillo said, "I've considered your offer, Señor Sand, and our nation would be happy to approve the proposed drilling..."

"That is good news, General."

"...for the minor consideration of one million dollars."

Sand groped for some appropriate response and found none, rather proud of himself for managing neither to laugh nor allow his mouth to drop open like a trap door. The offer he had sent from the hotel by messenger would trade twenty-five thousand dollars for this simple preliminary testing—more than Boldt Oil had paid for similar rights anywhere else in the world. General Trujillo had countered, also by messenger, with a ludicrous price of half a million dollars.

Sand had figured they would negotiate from there. Yesterday he had doubled his offer, again by messenger, and now here stood Trujillo doubling his own ridiculous figure.

Interesting negotiating tactic, Sand thought. *Just keep asking for more....*

Finally, Sand managed, "General Trujillo, if the test is successful, you may well make a million dollars, partnering with us. Likely much more. But that will be *after* we start pumping out oil. To ask for that kind of money when we don't even know with any certainty that there's oil down there? It's like demanding your winnings before the bet is even made."

Trujillo's grin was Cheshire cat worthy, and his demands just as absurd. "Señor Sand, I assure you, the oil is down there, just waiting to make all of us a fortune."

"Assurances are fine, sir, and I admire your confidence.

But an assurance on the open market is not worth a million dollars."

The General's smile remained, his expression otherwise blank, in part due to the impenetrably dark lenses of the sunglasses. "It is there. You have my word."

"Your word?"

The General responded with a single, slow-motion nod.

"And how do you know this, sir?"

That was apparently worth a shrug of only one shoulder. "I know this because we are standing here in my country, Señor. And I know everything there is to know about her. I would be an inferior leader if I did not."

Sand struggled to find a way to respond to Trujillo's lunatic style of transacting business without insulting the man. "I don't doubt that at all, General..."

"You are wise not to," Trujillo interjected.

Nodding, trying not to set the dictator off, Sand said, "Still, General, as a man of reason, you must surely appreciate my position. My company can't possibly make an investment of that scale on a test site."

The smile disappeared. "And *you*, Señor Sand, surely understand *our* position. Our growing nation needs the influx of cash that an oil company's generosity can bring."

Sand had noticed clusters of tar-paper shacks huddled next to the road on his way here, their thatched roofs in disrepair, their families firmly in poverty's grip. The despair they wallowed in was broken only by occasional patches of jungle. Perhaps this deal would help alleviate the hopelessness these people had suffered for too long. If he could get General Trujillo to sign on with Boldt Oil, and crude was actually discovered, thousands of jobs would open up for the locals.

But a million dollars?

There simply wasn't any way he could justify it.

With a smile and a nod, Sand said, "I'm sorry, General. Perhaps we can do business another day."

Trujillo's shrug had escalated to two shoulders. "We both know you will be back, Señor Sand, and when you return, the price will have doubled. Good day."

The dictator turned to the limousine; his chauffeur opened the door for him and Trujillo climbed in. As the vehicle pulled away raising dust, Sand was left wondering if the man was serious or if this was merely a bizarre style of negotiation. He watched as the limo disappeared into the distance, turning—somewhat surprisingly—away from the capital.

Then, shaking his head, Sand had climbed back into the rental car and was soon driving in the opposite direction.

That meeting was now an hour and some thirty kilometers behind him, and the only thing he seemed reasonably sure of for all his trouble was that Boldt Oil wouldn't be doing any test drilling in the Dominican Republic soon.

As the Chevy bounced along, Sand once again passed the tar-paper shacks and shook his head at how cavalierly their leader had turned down the opportunity to help lift his people from poverty.

The squalor trailed away as Sand approached the capital. Ciudad Trujillo rose rather grandly, new construction visible everywhere, most—in name at least—paying homage to Trujillo. Though no building could rise high enough to match the General's ego, the cool modern geometry of the growing skyline promised a better future.

Meanwhile, the relentless ancient heat of this place held Sand under its thumb. The city only seemed to exacerbate his discomfort, its crowded concrete walls holding the heat like an oven. This Caribbean island seemed far different than Jamaica, where he and Stacey had honeymooned almost a year ago. Where Kingston had been hot and breezy, the Dominican Republic tempered its searing heat with unbearable humidity. When it wasn't raining, the sun hammered the tiny country.

He couldn't remember feeling so punished by the weather even when he'd been an MI6 agent dispatched, it seemed, to every Godforsaken place on the planet. Even last year's Texas summer—a location he endured only because Stacey needed to live near her business holdings— had been cooler than this hothouse island.

As he entered the congestion of city traffic, Sand's pace slowed to a crawl. The car's vibration now subsided somewhat, though the heat, mixed with car and bus exhaust, washed over him like a sickly surf. Fighting nausea, he passed the time thinking about the cool shower that would await him when he returned to his hotel room.

Sand had confronted ruthless dictators before, the likes of whom made Trujillo look like St. Francis of Assisi; but nothing had prepared him for what he encountered today as vice president of a major oil company. Having leapt up the corporate ladder by marrying the boss, Sand found this position far more challenging than he could have expected, at least given his past employment history.

Reaching for his jacket on the passenger seat, he withdrew a handkerchief from a pocket and mopped his forehead. He thought about Stacey, forcing his mind away from the self-confident madman he'd encountered earlier. She had wanted him to retire completely, allow her to take care of all his needs. His pride had kept him from accepting that role.

After Trujillo, he wondered if perhaps she hadn't been right.

The thought of her brought a smile. Her sensual mouth, her green eyes, that wild auburn mane, she came rushing to him there in the car, the scent of her perfume heavy in his nostrils, washing away the stink of the city. He turned to see her sitting in the passenger seat, her creamy legs curled under her, her breasts rising and falling with her shallow breathing. The traffic melted away as he saw only Stacey....

The blaring horn of the truck behind him shook him from his revery. Glancing in the rear view, he saw the driver speaking to him in the universal sign language of all motorists. Sand waved sheepishly and inched the Chevy ahead the three feet that the other traffic had crawled while he daydreamed about Stacey. He laughed to himself—had it come to this? Fantasizing about his own wife? How sad. How wonderful.

They'd been married a year, during which they'd only been separated for two days, and Sand couldn't believe how much he missed the woman. *You're whipped, my friend,* a familiar voice in his head said. Yes, matrimony had changed him, but for the better he thought, though that inner voice remained skeptical.

After all, he'd never lasted more than six months in any man/woman relationship—not counting his service to the Queen, of course—and yet life with Stacey just seemed to be getting better and better. Why didn't more men marry incredibly beautiful, independently wealthy women?

Three black Fords occupied the spaces in front of the new twenty-story Hotel Trujillo. Sand was about to double park, leaving the rental for the valet, when he glanced into the first of the three black Fords and found it loaded with four serious-looking Latino men, one in the backseat failing to conceal a rifle, its barrel sticking up near the man's cheek.

Then, looking past the cars toward the hotel, Sand saw—exiting the lobby—a tall, mop-headed, skinny pock-marked man in an off-the-rack black suit...*George Glace!* Trying not to over-accelerate, Sand hit the gas and turned his head away as he rolled past the hotel and the remaining black Fords.

What was Glace, a freelance assassin often used by the CIA, doing coming out of a hotel in Ciudad Trujillo, with three matching black sedans waiting at the curb, each filled with rifle-wielding men? Were they lying in wait for him? To remove a cancer from the world?

No. Not "in wait"—just waiting.

The cadaverous assassin climbed into the rider's side of the lead Ford's front seat. Hairs at the back of Sand's neck prickled. Whipping the Chevy to the right, he started going around the block.

What was a CIA assassin doing in the Dominican Republic, backed up by a small army?

Other than extorting money from U.S. businesses—Boldt Oil a case in point—Trujillo was a dictator friendly to the United States.

Taking another right and gunning the car, Sand wondered if someone other than the CIA might be picking up Glace's tab—a political rival backed by another country, perhaps. It was a safe bet the killer wasn't here on vacation, and an equally safe wager Trujillo couldn't afford a hitman of Glace's caliber, so to speak. Sawing the wheel, Sand avoided a horse-drawn cart, then jerked the vehicle in the other direction to avoid a green Studebaker.

Sand revved the car around the third corner to a chorus of horns, inviting epithets in Spanish. His mind whirling with the possibilities, Sand stopped at the last corner of the square and watched the three Fords pull slowly away from the curb.

You're not a spy anymore, John, he reminded himself.

This was none of his business. Anyway, he was too knackered to play cowboys and Indians. A bloody shower was waiting! He should just let it drop....

Instead, Sand checked traffic, then turned right one last time and fell in three cars behind the Fords. Old habits died hard—retired or not, he simply couldn't walk away from Glace without knowing what the assassin was up to.

Following the cortege, the sun setting slowly to his left, Sand hung back, and soon found himself retracing his route back out of the city.

Ten minutes later—as darkness settled slowly over the island, the heat of the day hanging on like a last-call lover—Sand barely made out the taillights of the final car in line as it braked quickly and pulled off the road into a familiar access lane into the jungle.

And, of course, he knew.

Glace and his band of merry men planned to ambush Trujillo as the General returned to the city. Sand didn't know how, but he intended to stop them. Whether he liked the dictator or not—and of course he didn't—having the General out of the game would hardly guarantee a better deal for Boldt Oil. In a banana republic like this, the next leader might be even more around the bend. Sand, and Boldt, couldn't afford to take that chance.

Or maybe Sand was just bored.

Behind him, the blackness of night engulfed the empty ribbon of blacktop. After killing his headlights, and pulling into the access road, Sand cut the engine and let the car coast to a quiet halt without using the brakes. He stepped from the vehicle, got behind it and unlocked the boot, from which he took his shoulder-holstered Walther from its hiding place behind the spare tire. Also tucked back there was the Walther's silencer, which he attached to the weapon.

Making your way through the underbrush in complete darkness was something of a trick, but one Sand had performed before, and fairly often. He navigated himself with ease to the edge of the small clearing where the black Ford had parked in knee-high grass. The driver still sat behind the wheel, a cigarette in his left hand, elbow out the window, curls of smoke rising. The other three stood in a semi-circle on the passenger side, just a few yards away, their backs to Sand, cigarettes in one hand, rifles gripped loosely in the other.

They were chatting, and Sand soon had picked up on their names: the skinny one at left was Julio, the short, plump middle one Carlos, and on the right burly Raúl.

Briefly, Sand considered shooting the three where they stood, giving them no time to react, and taking his chances with the driver. Though his silencer would keep the sound of the gunshots from carrying too far on the night air, the driver likely had a walkie-talkie to communicate with Glace's other cars and would raise an alarm before Sand could deal with him.

Sand realized, of course, that as a retired intelligence officer he no longer had the authority in the field to, at his discretion, terminate with extreme prejudice, which his writer friend had glibly termed a license to kill. Being the executive vice president of Boldt Oil did not carry with it any such privilege.

This would be viewed as murder by the American government, although certainly General Trujillo would be grateful for Sand's efforts, with no one else the wiser. Should improve Boldt's bargaining position....

The attack would have to be quiet, precise, pitiless.

Sweat trickled down his forehead, dripped into his eyes as he lay there, prone in the jungle grass, mosquitos nibbling at his hands and face, his soaked shirt sticking to his back. John Sand had never felt more at home.

The driver would have to go first.

Sand crawled to his left, then circled toward the car, inching steadily forward, keeping the Ford between himself and the other three assassins. On hands and knees, he crept to just behind the driver's door. Taking a fountain pen from his shirt pocket, he uncapped what instantly became a makeshift knife and waited until the driver flipped his cigarette butt out the window.

Sand popped up and reached his left hand in and clasped it over the driver's mouth, pushing the man's head back, and jammed the sharp end of the pen into his carotid artery. Through the car windows, he could see that the others hadn't turned his way as beneath his hand the shuddering driver's gasps were muffled into murmur, until the subject went slack.

Took under a minute.

He left the writing instrument sticking out of the man's neck, cutting off any blood spurt, and now—with the driver's heart stopped—no blood flow of any kind would follow, other than a stray dribble.

Good.

Sliding back down the side of the car, Sand crawled to the rear bumper. The other three assassins had moved off a few more feet to the left, so that two of them—Julio and Carlos—could plop onto a big squat stump, their backs still to him, while Raúl had stepped to their rear and parallel to where Sand was hiding in the grass. The muscular-looking assassin began to relieve himself, his sigh almost orgasmic, his rifle leaning against him.

Crawling closer, Sand moved behind the man who was pissing into the grass, still doing that when Sand came up behind him and reached his left hand around to cover the man's mouth while shoving the snout of the weapon right up against his spine, further muffling the silenced bullet that went through him.

You were holding the wrong gun, mate, Sand thought.

When Sand eased the corpse down, and slipped back deep in the grass, the two men at the stump heard something and turned their heads toward where they'd seen their comrade wander off, not seeing him now. Julio got to his feet, rifle raised in that direction, while fat Carlos remained seated, smoking his cigarette.

From the underbrush, Sand shot Julio in the head, gore flying into the grass, the skinny assassin falling backward onto his brains. The terrified Carlos was looking behind him, wide-eyed, thinking about going for the rifle leaned against the squat stump.

Sand got to his feet. "No," he said.

No was no in any language.

Carlos stared into the bottomless hole that began at the tip of the Walther and ended at eternity, and—dropping his cigarette—he pushed his rifle away.

Sand came slowly over and around to face the plump killer, asking, "*Habla ingles?*"

Carlos shook his head.

Sand shot the stump between Carlos' legs, chewing bark.

Carlos jumped as if touched by a cattle prod.

"*Habla ingles?*" Sand repeated.

Nodding, his hands up, Carlos said, "*Poquito.*"

A little bit.

"What were you boys up to?"

Carlos frowned in thought, possibly trying to translate Sand's words or maybe just looking for an answer that might not get him killed. His eyes darted to his fallen companion, then back to Sand. A shrug.

Sand thumbed back the Walther's hammer; in a jungle filled with sinister sounds, this was the loudest and most sinister.

"You aren't going to make me ask you again, are you?"

Carlos shook his head. "If I tell you, he will kill me."

"Glace?"

"...Sí."

"Sí, he would kill you. But Glace is not here, and I am... and if you don't talk, *I* will kill you now."

Sneaking a peek at his dead partner, head cushioned in gore, Carlos took in a deep breath and slowly let it out.

"The General. We assassinate the General."

"Trujillo."

"Sí."

"What is the plan?"

Carlos shook his head again.

Firing the pistol, Sand splintered off a piece of the stump Benny perched on, right where his now late friend had not long ago been sitting.

Carlos jumped, then spoke quickly. "We are only...how do you say *el apoyo*?"

"The backup," Sand said.

"Sí. If somehow the General live through the...*fuego cruzado*?"

"Crossfire."

"*Fuego cruzado* up the road, we step in."

Sand swore under his breath. That damned Glace had never been less than thorough. Now he had to catch up with those other two cars, but first he must get rid of Carlos. The plump assassin seemed to sense this and slowly crossed himself and began to pray.

"Get up," Sand said. "Move away from there."

Carlos did as he was told, his lips still active with silent prayer. His eyes were filled with tears. Even assassins had feelings, at least for themselves.

"Turn around."

Again, Carlos did so.

Sand cracked Carlos behind the ear with the barrel of the Walther, probably not hard enough to kill him. The killer dropped to the ground like a sack of grain.

Hurrying back to his rented Chevy, Sand wondered how exactly he expected to stop eight armed assassins positioned to catch the Dominican dictator in their crossfire. He had his answer before he got the Chevy started—not the answer he wanted, but an answer, all right.

Perhaps two kilometers down the road oncoming headlights cut through the night. As the car drew nearer, muzzle flashes from either side preceded the rifle reports. This lasted less than thirty seconds, but even from this distance, Sand knew that Glace and his operatives had accomplished their mission.

What this meant for Boldt Oil's efforts to test drill in the Dominican Republic, Sand couldn't guess. But the job of an executive vice president was turning out to be an interesting way to leave the dangerous life of a secret agent behind.

CHAPTER FOUR
THE BROTHER-IN-LAWFORD

Stacey's one-piece bathing suit was a sky-blue print bearing a scattering of red roses, as if they'd been tossed in the air and randomly landed here and there on her shapely frame. Under the bright sunshine, her deeply tanned flesh made her auburn hair, worn shorter now, blowing free in the breeze, appear almost blonde by way of contrast.

Her green eyes drilled into him as she walked down the steps to join him in the pool.

"I believe I'll tear those trunks right off you," she said, "and have my way."

Sand's laugh caught in its throat, as it often did when she talked to him like a man. Standing in the shallow to his waist, he backed slowly toward the deep end of the pool, until only his shoulders and head were above water.

As he went, he taunted, "You wouldn't dare."

She followed him on her toes and kept her chin above water as the bottom began to drop away. "Don't make me chase you—you're only going to make it harder on yourself."

"You're already making it harder for me."

He'd been home a week.

For two days, he'd withheld from Stacey what he'd done the night of Trujillo's assassination, not caring to make her an accessory after the fact. But when he'd thought about it, he came to the conclusion that no government on earth—not the United States nor the República Dominicana—was likely to bring any charges against him...even if the bodies of those assassins had been connected to him, which as far as he knew wasn't the case.

So he'd told her. Chapter and verse.

She had been outraged, but not over the killings themselves, rather the dangers and ramifications.

"You are supposed to be *retired* from such things," she all but screamed. "What in God's name did you think you were *doing?* Did you consider what effect this would've had on Boldt Oil if you'd been caught? Or what effect getting yourself killed would have on the woman who loves you?"

He had no reply.

"Goddamnit, John Sand! You are the most self-centered son of a bitch it's ever been my misfortune to meet."

And she'd stormed out.

Ever since then, things had been a little tense—nothing major. No worse than the Americans and their new Cuban neighbors.

And for the first time in a year of marriage, they had not made love at least once a day, excluding of course his time away to the Dominican Republic. They had not, in fact, made love for the four days since he'd finally shared the details of the Caribbean episode with her. Slept in the same bed, yes, but with Stacey on her side, her back to him, until two nights ago, when he decamped to the guest room.

Now, standing in the pool, teetering on the brink of

the deep, he watched as his smiling bride swam slowly toward him, like a shark who'd spotted a helpless meal that required no special rush.

Taking one more backward step, bringing the water to his chin, Sand grinned as Stacey leapt at him, her slim curves creating a wake that might have drowned a lesser man as she wrapped her arms around him and dragged him under. He struggled not to laugh or inhale, then he felt a new freedom as his trunks slipped down around his thighs, knees, ankles, and were gone.

The first sound he heard when he broke the surface was Stacey's laughter. Coughing, he shook the water from his eyes and followed what were now giggles to the shallow end. Grabbing her, he tried to pull her under, to give her back some of her own; but somehow she slithered through his arms as he went down, swallowing another chlorine-flavored mouthful as his knees scraped the bottom.

More cautious as he surfaced this time, Sand wiped his face with wet hands, hacked up more water, then stared at his wife where she sat at the end of the shallow section on the pool's edge, gently kicking.

"Lose something?" she asked, a wicked grin playing at the corners of her mouth as she glanced at his sopping trunks in a pile next to her.

"Only my dignity."

She shrugged. "You Brits highly overrate dignity, I think."

He walked slowly through the water toward her, sloshing. "I suppose we do."

"I might have something to soothe the loss."

"Really?"

"Really."

Still seated at pool's edge, she used her right hand to

slip the strap of her bathing suit over her left shoulder, then used her left hand to tug down the strap at her right shoulder. Her thumbs brought the damp cloth down over, and freeing, her full alabaster breasts, the nipples at attention.

As was he.

She stood, tugged the suit off the rest of the way, let it puddle at her feet, and then walked saucily through the glass doors into the kitchen of the modern wing of the big Boldt mansion, taking a turn to the left toward the guest bedroom.

His current digs.

"Apparently," he said to himself, "I'm forgiven."

Half an hour later, they were outdoors again, with glasses of iced tea at a poolside table under an umbrella, their swim togs recovered and both in terrycloth robes that ended mid-thigh. The identical nature of the garments somehow underscored the equality of their relationship. At least to him it did, and he didn't mind at all.

She said, "We won't belabor this."

"Splendid."

"But you are an executive now. We share responsibility for running a company that thousands of employees depend upon for their livelihoods, and which our respective governments depend upon for a steady supply of energy."

"You have a steady supply of energy yourself, I've noticed."

She gave him a pixie smile, but it did not include her green eyes, which seemed to burn into him. "You cannot react to situations as if you were still working for MI6. It's personally and professionally dangerous."

He nodded.

"I can't have you out there," she said, and her expression softened, "alone...getting yourself into....Can't have that."

There was something puzzling here. In a sense, she did not appear to be so much upset over what *he'd* done, but that she'd not been a part of it—at his side to pitch in. On the face of it, such a notion was crazy, yet hadn't she got a thrill out of their adventure in Jamaica? She had said as much, more than once, in this year since their memorable honeymoon.

He didn't know the answer, but he knew the subject would come up again. In a life or death situation, he would revert—he *knew* he would—to the man he'd been for so many years, the man who would always make sure the death in such situations was someone else's. But now did not seem to be the proper time to take this discussion any further.

The doorbell rang inside the house, distant but distinct.

"I'll get it," she said.

"Rich people don't answer their own doors," Sand reminded her.

"They do when the help has the day off."

"Ah. Rough it then. Answer it yourself."

She did.

***

As the doorbell chimed a second time, Stacey moved through the modern wing into the older, larger house with its rustic trappings that were both homey and antique, walking down the central hall, past the living room with its cowhide throw rug and the framed oil portrait of her father over the fireplace. The trip was long enough to require patience from their caller, although not enough so to prevent a third try at the bell.

She opened the door, by now a little annoyed by the insistence of that bell, only to look up into the blue eyes and handsome features of Peter Lawford, the British-born, American-based actor, an unexpected guest famous enough to leave the former Stacey Boldt speechless.

Sporting a navy blazer, white open-at-the-throat shirt, and white trousers with matching shoes, he made a presence at once striking and friendly. His black hair, swept back, gray at the temples, contrasted with the overwhelming white of his apparel, as did his deeply tanned face and hands. Obviously, he'd spent a lot of time in the sun, at least recently.

He stared at her for a moment, politely waiting for her to say something, anything, and when she didn't, he finally said, "I'm terribly sorry, but would this be the home of Mr. John Sand?"

Frozen in the manner so many assume when unexpectedly encountering a celebrity, Stacey only managed a nod.

The half-smile was effortlessly charming. "Would he be about?"

"...About what?"

"The, uh, house. Would he be available?"

"You're Peter Lawford."

He flashed the full famous smile. "I have been for some time now. It's rather automatic at this point."

"I'm sorry, Mr. Lawford," Stacey said, embarrassed, and she opened the big heavy door wider. "Won't you come in?"

"I don't wish to intrude. But might I see Mr. Sand? There's a purpose for my call, but also he and I go back a rather long way."

"Well, you're both from England," she said, a remark she knew at once was ridiculous, as if everyone in that country would obviously be acquainted. She composed herself. "You're welcome here, Mr. Lawford. Come in, come in."

He did. He did.

"I'm Stacey, John's wife."

"Ah!" Lawford reached out, took her hand, brought it slowly to his lips and kissed the back of it, returning it all the better for the trip. "A pleasure to meet you, Mrs. Sand... Stacey. And what a fortunate man your husband is."

Stacey felt the blush taking her cheeks and might have kicked herself for it. She ran a Fortune 500 company, had met billionaires, world leaders, assorted celebrities, and had even been shot at on her honeymoon by a megalomaniac's minion. Yet it appeared she was unable to carry on a simple conversation with one British-American actor.

But she did manage, "John's out by the pool. We can join him there."

"Thank you, Mrs. Sand."

"Stacey. I insist."

That smile again. "Stacey....When did you and John tie the knot?"

As she led Lawford through the house, she told him about their simple wedding, their Port Royal honeymoon (leaving out the sex and violence), and their move to Houston to be near her business holdings. And of course that John was retired from his former work for the British government and now a Texas oil executive.

"Deep in the heart of," Lawford said lightly.

"Deep in my heart, at least," she said, finally at ease with the actor, who made that not at all hard.

***

When Stacey and their caller stepped through the glass doors onto the patio, Sand—still with his iced tea at the umbrella table—couldn't make him out at first, the glare of sunlight making it impossible, despite the ex-agent's Ray-Bans.

Stacey threw her mate a look that at once indicated she was impressed by the nature of his acquaintances but also was wondering just what in the world this could be about.

As was Sand.

Rising to come around the table, the man of the house gave this unanticipated guest a smile and his hand. "Peter, old man, how the hell have you been?"

Lawford ignored the hand and enveloped Sand in a bear hug. "John, it's marvelous to see you. You do look fit! You would *have* to, to ensnare a woman like this."

Was Stacey blushing? That wasn't like her....

"Thank you, Peter. You, too. You've been getting some sun. Nassau?"

"Kanab."

Sand blinked. "Where in the Caribbean is that?"

"Nowhere in the Caribbean. Utah. Southern Utah, to be exact—near Arizona. Filming there, old boy."

Stacey came to Sand's side and slipped an arm around her husband's waist. There was something vaguely accusatory in her tone as she said, "You never mentioned having such a famous friend, dear."

Lawford said, "What's marriage without a few surprises? Besides, I'm quite sure John knows any number of people more famous than a certain child actor going slowly to seed."

She looked from one to the other. "Where do you two know each other from?"

Lawford's grin was winningly shy. "We went to school together, Stacey. Quite a long time ago."

A lie, but one Sand gladly went along with.

He was well aware that Lawford had always felt embarrassed by a lack of formal education, his snobbish mother having schooled her son through tutors trailing the globe-hopping family. Though Lady Lawford loved to put on airs and bask in the attention that came with her station, the truth was she had cheated on her first husband and allowed herself to get pregnant in order to land Lord Sydney Lawford and the title she so coveted.

Worried about whispers and rumors in a barely post-Victorian England, Lady Lawford had kept the family on the go. They flitted between the States, Australia, the Bahamas, India, Tasmania, Tahiti, Colombia, Cuba, Panama, and Europe. Referring to this nomadic childhood, Lawford had once told Sand, "I loved it and it never occurred to me that it might be an odd way to grow up."

Sand's own childhood had been far less worldly. Raised in a small town northwest of London, he had met Lawford when the eight-year-old aspiring actor's mother took the train to the Sand family's native Borehamwood and hired Sand's father to taxi the Lawfords to Elstree, the so-called "British Hollywood" a few kilometers away.

The two boys, not that different in age, had hit it off and became fast friends, despite seeing each other somewhat rarely over the following ten years. It was as adults, both men frequently far away from Britain, that the friendship had truly blossomed.

"We've seen each other a good number of times over the years," Sand said, "but not for...what now, Peter? Five years?"

"Nearly so."

Stacey, having taken all that in, said, "I'm sorry, where are my manners? Peter, would you like something to drink?"

"Gin and tonic would suit," he said.

"Vodka martini, John?"

"Of course," he said.

Lawford, teasingly, asked, "Shaken not stirred?'

"Do I care?"

She made that happen at the nearby cart, including two fingers of Jim Beam on the rocks for herself (her daddy's favorite), and soon the three had settled around the umbrella-sheltered table to make small talk. It was pleasant enough for Sand, but he knew that Peter was not a "drop by" sort of individual, particularly not during a film shoot several states away.

Finally Lawford tossed Sand a casual look that the former intelligence man nonetheless immediately understood.

"Stacey, darling," Sand said, "I believe there's a lime in the refrigerator. Would you be a good girl and cut it up for us, for the next round?"

She rose, smiled at them, obviously aware she'd been asked to make herself scarce for a while, but—as a "good girl"—taking no offense, saying, "I would do the same for any movie star guest of yours, darling."

She walked across the patio, doing wonders for terry-cloth.

Both men watched her disappear into the house.

"You lucky bastard," Lawford said, then bent close to his old friend and spoke in low tones, rapid fire. "John, I'm here on behalf of the President."

"Of the United States, I trust?" Sand asked lightly, although his question hardly needed an answer. The actor had married the current American president's sister back in 1954, an event at which Sand had been one of the groomsmen.

Lawford twitched a smile, but his eyes frowned. "He needs you and your...shall we call them....unique talents?"

Sand glanced toward the glass doors, behind which Stacey worked in the kitchen. "I would think he would have sufficient access to men with my 'talents' who are active agents and are part of his own government. The CIA, for instance."

Lawford shrugged. "I can't answer that. I only know that he asked me to reach out to you. He says he needs you. At the very least, he wants to see you, to talk to you. It's important. And it's top secret, as they say."

"What am I to tell Stacey?"

"Nothing. No one must know."

Sand shook his head. "I promised her I wouldn't engage in my previous line of work."

Lawford said, firmly, rather formally, "The President of the United States has dispatched me to ask for your assistance."

"I'm not even a citizen."

"But you're my friend! Also, last time I looked, England is still an ally."

That got a chuckle out of Sand, but then he took several moments to consider, his eyes on those glass doors and the small figure at work carrying out his silly errand.

Then he said, "I'll talk to the man, but more than that I can't promise."

Lawford patted his old friend on the arm. "Good enough for me. Now. He'll meet you in Kanab tomorrow afternoon."

Startled, Sand said, "Where? When?"

"Must I repeat myself?"

Sand was shaking his head. "Stacey will never let me go to Utah to a film set with you, and not take her."

"*Let* you?" Lawford chuckled. "Are you really *already* that whipped, old boy?"

Lawford echoing his own thoughts threw Sand a bit, underscored by the re-emergence from the house of Stacey, bearing the cut-up lime on a saucer.

"I'll never understand you Brits and your gin and tonics," she said mock-scoldingly. "Why can't you drink whiskey like normal folks?"

Sand said, "One hundred eighty years later, and she's still fighting the crown."

"And winning," she said with a sly smile, joining them at the table. She turned her attention to their guest. "I don't suppose you two would like to share what you were talking about when you sent me off to do my wifely duty."

The two men exchanged a glance.

The actor flashed that winning smile. "I was asking your husband's permission to surprise you."

"Oh, really, and did he grant it?"

"Well, he said he'd leave it up to you. From everything I can gather, you seem to be in charge here at El Rancho Boldt."

Stacey nodded. "I'm glad that's been established. What surprise is it you wanted to spring?"

Lawford paused dramatically to take a sip of his gin and tonic, now dressed with a slice of lime. "Just wondering if you'd care to meet Frank and the boys."

Stacey's face lit up. "Frank? As in Sinatra?"

"Yes. And Dean and Sammy and Joey too."

Sand said, "Who wouldn't be thrilled to meet Joey Bishop?"

Stacey said, "You wouldn't kid a girl?"

"No, or a full-grown married woman either," Lawford said. "When Frank learned I was buddies with the inspiration for you-know-who, he just *had* to meet the real thing."

She looked at her husband, "Did you say yes?"

"No."

"No!"

"You heard the man. I said it was up to you."

She threw her arms around Sand's neck and kissed him.

Lawford asked, "May I take *that* as a 'yes'?"

"You may!" She kissed Sand again.

Lawford said, "You do know I'm the one who put this in motion."

She came over and slung her arms around their guest's neck and gave him a big smooch.

Just as Sand had said, but with entirely different inflection, she asked, "Where? When?"

"Tomorrow," the actor said. "In Kanab, Utah. We're making a film there."

Her eyebrows went up. "In that location, it must be a western."

He nodded. "Cavalry movie. *Sergeants 3*. A take-off on the old *Gunga Din*."

Sand sat back, sipping his vodka martini, watching Stacey quiz Peter about his famous friends. His mind was elsewhere, fixed upon the question of why President Kennedy would want to see him. He knew it wasn't to hear the real stories behind the exaggerations, however much JFK might enjoy those puffed-up fantasies.

Stacey brought Sand back with a question: "Can you believe we're going to meet the Rat Pack, darlin'?"

"I am struggling to contain myself," Sand said as dry as his martini.

The actor's grin turned sheepish. "Only the reporters call us that. Frank says we're 'The Clan.' I find that in questionable taste, actually. But since Sammy doesn't seem to mind, who am I to complain?"

CHAPTER FIVE

DESERT SUMMIT

After hopping Boldt Oil's private plane to Las Vegas, the Sands and Peter Lawford rode for hours in the compromised comfort of a Lincoln, its air-conditioning turned on only occasionally. Much of the drive took them down cowpath dirt roads that even a limo couldn't navigate without considerable jostling. But that only seemed to make Stacey's anticipation grow, as they neared their desert destination.

Though she'd grown up a daughter of wealth, and had met more than her share of the rich and famous, Stacey had never been on a movie set, nor had she met any show business personalities on the level of fame enjoyed by Frank, Dean, Sammy, and Peter. The closest she'd come had been when her late father introduced her to Ronald Reagan, who had been in Houston to film a Boldt Oil promotional spot; but a faded forties movie star was hardly on the Rat Pack's level. Not even Joey Bishop's.

Beside her in the backseat, John seemed atypically tense, eyes straight ahead as Maury, Sinatra's vaguely thuggish driver, maneuvered this last stretch of questionable road. The world outside was a hostile one, temperature hovering in the high nineties, visible through the haze of dust stirred by the vehicle.

"We can only run the air conditioner a little while at a time," heavyset Maury had warned them when they climbed into the black Lincoln. "It really eats the gas and there's nowhere to fill up out here in the sticks."

But it had been half an hour since the last friendly blast of cool air, and Stacey's white silk blouse felt like the second skin a snake might be trying to shed.

She asked, "Couldn't we turn the air conditioner back on for a few minutes?"

Flipping the switch, Maury said, "Guess we can risk it."

Peter, in the rider's seat up front, looked back with his smile turned up to full wattage. "We're almost there, Stacey. Not much longer now."

She said to her husband, "You're quiet even for you. Surely you're not nervous about meeting the Chairman of the Board?"

"Who?"

"That's what they're calling Mr. Sinatra now—'The Voice' is old hat."

His glance told her she might just as well have been speaking Esperanto.

Peter glanced back again. "The moniker has to do with him starting Reprise Records earlier this year. But he doesn't care to be called that, particularly."

"I will resist the urge," John said. And to Stacey, he said, "No case of nerves, dear. Just busy enjoying the scenery."

Staring straight ahead at the dust they were raising?

Stacey huffed a laugh. "A holiday on Mars, all rocks and dirt."

"Not entirely true. This terrain has its charms."

Her husband wasn't wrong. Arid though it was, Monument Valley was blessed with ruggedly carved mountains, exotic if sparse vegetation, and a startlingly blue sky. In Texas she had been in locales just as dry, of course, but no scenery as striking.

"Welcome to Kanab," Peter announced as they passed a city limits sign and cut through a cluster of motels and gas stations.

"Fourteen hundred," John said. "Your average Vegas casino has a bigger population."

Lawford met John's eyes in the rearview mirror. "When you go to the Dairy Queen, best request two scoops, as there's nothing to do once it closes."

"That sounds more like Bishop," John said, with a slight smile, "than Lawford."

"A paraphrase."

They were passing through a low-slung nondescript few blocks of business district with the occasional pick-up truck parked on either side among the few signs of life.

Stacey asked, "Why choose a bump in the road like this for a base of operations?"

Lawford said, "Your hubby's implication is correct—the director wanted to get our rowdy little band as far away from Vegas as possible, I think. Additionally, some forty western movies have made Kanab their home away from home. The town's Hollywood ties go back to the Twenties."

Soon they were easing to a stop in a graveled lot shared with a cluster of recreational vehicles. Perhaps a hundred yards farther on, what seemed to be a frontier Army fort rose out of the dusty valley like a mirage of the past.

"The boys will be down at the fort by now," Lawford said as the car rolled to a stop in a graveled lot. "We're scheduled to shoot there all day."

They exited the limo, stretched, and bid Maury good-bye, then followed Peter's lead, ambling toward the fort.

"Should you need to freshen up," Peter said, "the honeywagon's just off to the right of Fort Sinatra."

"Honeywagon?" Stacey asked.

"Portable W.C.," her husband explained. He paused, grimacing, and put a hand on his stomach. "Anything closer? I'm afraid I have a rather pressing matter to deal with."

Stacey frowned at John, who normally had a cast-iron stomach, though their quick breakfast at the airport had admittedly been on the greasy side.

"That's my trailer there," Lawford said, nodding to the left. "Rather more modest compared to Frank's and Dean's, I'm afraid. But my facilities should suffice."

Two men in sunglasses and dark suits were standing at either side of the few steps up to the RV's door. *Security, probably,* Stacey thought. But why suits and ties in this climate, and standing guard at a portable dressing room when the cast and crew seemed to be at work at the fort?

John said, "You two go ahead. Afraid I may be a while."

Stacey, mildly concerned, asked, "Are you all right, dear?"

"Seem to have picked up a bug. Go on—I'll find you."

Peter lightly teased, "You don't seem to be as impervious to human frailties as the super spy in the books."

"My writer friend leaves those parts out," John said with half a smile.

But Stacey found this entire exchange a little odd, even troubling, as she fell in step with the actor and headed for the fort.

***

As he walked toward the trailer, Sand could feel his wife's eyes on him, but didn't glance back. He kept a steady pace as he approached the two men, who were expecting him yet acknowledged him not at all.

They shared the bland, instantly forgettable features common to their trade, distinguishable only by the blond hair at left and red hair at right. Both seemed in shape, if not overly muscular, their dark suits tailored to make invisible any weapon bulge.

Utah was every bit as hot as the Dominican Republic, perhaps even hotter, but the desert didn't have the punishing humidity. Utah was, comparatively, a breath of fresh air. Now Sand glanced toward the receding Stacey and Lawford.

"Sir," the redhead said.

"Afternoon, gentleman."

"You needn't lift your arms high," the blond said. "We'll make this quick."

He raised his hands to his rib cage, the redhead's frisk quick and efficient. Glancing over his shoulder, Sand was glad to see the backs of Stacey and Lawford, the pair well on their way—he would hate to have to explain the necessity of being searched before a bathroom break.

"Please go in, sir," the redhead said.

Sand nodded and climbed two aluminum stairs, then knocked on the trailer door.

The voice within was muffled, distant. "Come in."

Inside, Sand took a moment to adjust from the bright sun to the relative darkness. Lawford's RV was not at all spacious and definitely not good enough for Frank Sinatra—paneled in sickly orange-ish wood with an aquamarine dining nook tucked to the right, a mini-kitchen to the left, past which you accessed a tiny loo off to the right and, at the rear, an aqua couch spanned the narrows walls looking terribly uncomfortable and probably opening into an even more uncomfortable sleeping accommodation.

The fortyish man seated on that couch rose immediately, if with a little difficulty, slender, handsome, instantly recognizable, though his apparel—blue polo and white slacks—was more Cape Cod sloop than Oval Office.

The President of the United States whipped off and tossed aside a pair of horn-rimmed reading glasses, which were hardly the American Optical Saratoga sunglasses for which he was noted and imitated. He'd been working on a stack of files that were next to where he'd been seated. His greenish-gray eyes alive with energy, John Fitzgerald Kennedy approached with his hand extended.

Sand took it and returned the President's firm grip.

"Thank you for coming, Mr. Sand."

"A pleasure to see you, Mr. President."

"I have coffee waiting. Or do you prefer tea?"

"In America, I take coffee. Wasn't it Thomas Jefferson who said coffee was the favorite drink of the civilized world?"

That famous grin flashed. "If he didn't, he should have."

Sand's host gestured to the dining nook, where Styrofoam cups of coffee indeed waited, with packaged cream and sugar in a dish, of which neither man partook. Sand noted that Kennedy had a bit of trouble getting comfortable in the space age bench of the little booth; but then anyone would.

"I'm something of a fan of yours, these days," Kennedy said. "But of course you know that."

"Don't believe everything you read."

Another grin. "I won't if you won't."

The nook's tabletop was also home to a half-filled ashtray, a pack of Peter's cigarettes, and a round, brass lighter about the size of a cricket ball.

Kennedy said, "John—may I call you John?"

They'd only met once before, and it had been at Peter's wedding, very briefly. And of course the President of the United States could call him anything.

Sand nodded, but did not request the same liberty. Besides which, one John per conversation was quite enough.

"John, uh, the reason I've asked you here is a matter of the utmost secrecy and, uh, of the utmost concern to the security of the United States."

That sounded ominous. Sand said nothing.

"Let me say, I know a lot about you, and I am not referring to your, uh, former colleague's entertaining novels. I'm familiar with a number of your missions, to the extent your intelligence service was willing to share them, and in general with your exemplary service to your nation."

"Thank you, sir."

After a sip of coffee, Kennedy said, "But you have a *new* country now, John—you're a prospective immigrant by marriage, green card and all."

"I am indeed."

What came next was perhaps too casual: "Well, your new home needs your help. Are you, uh, willing?"

Definitely something ominous in the air.

"I am willing to listen," Sand conceded.

The President's hands moved constantly as he spoke, emphasizing a point, pounding a rhythm on the tabletop. "I need to get into some confidential areas, John. I am not, uh, going to ask you to sign off on anything officially, but I want your word."

"You have it."

"Good. Then let's start with Trujillo."

"You mean his assassination."

"Yes," Kennedy said.

"It was your work."

The color drained from the President's face. "That's not true."

"I was there, sir," Sand said, matter of fact.

Kennedy's tone bordered on defensive. "I am aware you were in the Dominican Republic at the time, but, uh, what your role may have been is...conjecture. Just as your assumption that the assassination was my, uh....What exactly did you see, John?"

"I saw Glace. Exactly."

Sand had expected that name to have an impact, but it did not—only confusion played on the President's face. Or was he just a good actor, at least as good as the man whose trailer they occupied?

"Who or what is 'Glace'?" Kennedy asked. "Is that a name?

"Yes, of an assassin who works frequently for your CIA."

The President paused, then nodded slowly, which seemed significant in a man of such energy. "Which is why you assume I ordered the assassination of General Trujillo."

Sand decided to view that as a rhetorical question.

"I didn't," his host said.

"If you say so, sir."

Kennedy's fist came down on the tabletop and the coffee cups and ashtray jumped. "I *do* say so, John. Damn it, man. That's the problem that brings you here! It's why I'm talking to an MI6 agent—a former one, as opposed to someone currently active."

An awkward pause was broken when Sand said, "You suspect the CIA is operating behind your back. And you've run out of people you feel you can trust."

"That is the situation. You seem a viable option. You were the best in your field of, uh, work who qualified."

"The operative word there is 'were,' Mr. President. I have been retired from intelligence 'work' for nearly two years. I am an oil company executive these days, as perhaps you're aware."

Something sly crept into a corner of the President's mouth. "But you've, uh, kept your hand in, haven't you?"

"Sir?"

"That conjecture I referred to, which came from CIA sources, assembling their so-called facts concerning General Trujillo's death...I'm told that part of the assassination team got taken out by some unknown party. A party with considerable skills in your former occupation."

"Interesting information, if vague."

The green eyes drilled into him. "Are you saying that *wasn't* your work?"

Sand paused for a sip of coffee, then said, "That's a violent part of the world with many players knowledgeable in my...specialty."

"You just confirmed you were there."

Sand flipped a hand. "Representing Boldt Oil, trying to make a deal with Trujillo for drilling rights. Nothing remotely to do with his assassination."

"Except, perhaps, trying to prevent it? So that, uh, a major business deal would not die with him?"

"Frankly, we weren't even *close* to a deal."

Kennedy's frustration was apparent. He was not a man used to have someone defy him who, under any other circumstances, would be his subordinate.

"John," Kennedy said, "you are understandably reluctant to speak frankly. This camper could be wired. But let me say two things. First, I do not generally handle tradecraft personally, such as entrapment efforts and intelligence operations. Second, I guarantee you that everything we say here is off the record. It *has* to be. For my needs *and* yours."

"Fine," Sand said." Then I'd like to start with a question on a particularly sensitive subject."

"All right."

"The Bay of Pigs."

"What about it?"

"Did you order the invasion?"

The air seemed to go out of his famous host. "That's, uh, a really unnecessary question to pose, don't you think, John? I've already taken responsibility in the press."

"The buck stops here, I believe the expression goes."

"It does."

Shrugging, Sand said, "Now, after you've taken responsibility for this embarrassing farrago, you feel you can't trust anyone around you...so you call me. But, Mr. President, why should I trust you? Did you actually *order* the invasion...or just cover up for those who did?"

For several moments that seemed much longer, the two men stared at each other.

Finally, Kennedy said, "Ike okayed the plan back in 1960. After the inauguration, I, uh, inherited the plan. Castro had been getting arms shipments from the Russians, and a free Cuba seemed the only way for us to stay safe. So, yes—I *ordered* the Bay Of Pigs invasion. My call. My responsibility. Now, what the hell really happened in the Dominican Republic?"

Sand told him.

At the conclusion of Sand's frank and factual report, the President said, "John, I reiterate. I knew nothing about any plans to assassinate Trujillo."

"And, of course, I can take that at face value, since no American president in history has ever lied."

Instead of displaying anger, Kennedy sat back against the uncomfortable space-age plastic seating and laughed heartily—a joyful sound that made Sand smile.

"That was a good one, John—I do love that understated British humor."

Kennedy had apparently never been to a music hall.

"But the truth," the President was saying, "is that I had nothing to do with the Trujillo killing. In fact, I can't imagine why you or anyone else would even *think* that we would be behind it. He was friendly to our cause."

"If you didn't feel forces within your own government were responsible, all due respect, you wouldn't have summoned me."

The President's nod was slight but spoke volumes. "I do think we were linked to it, somehow...but only because I believe the CIA has, uh, its own agenda. Or at least rogue agents within the agency do, working without the knowledge of either the Executive branch or Congress. I'm just trying to, uh, get to the bottom of this goddamn thing, starting with...why would the CIA want Trujillo dead?"

Sand shrugged. "It might well be the oil."

"The drilling rights you were there negotiating."

"Precisely...but Trujillo was a lunatic. At every stage of the negotiation, the price doubled. Boldt Oil could hardly be the only company to run into the General's barking-mad negotiating style."

Kennedy swallowed coffee, then said, "Any one of Boldt's competitors could well afford a professional killer...but why use someone so closely tied to the CIA?"

Sand's eyebrows rose. "If the CIA was involved, they

would need a reason."

The President nodded.

Sand continued: "If an oil company—or secret consortium of oil companies—underwrote the assassination, the CIA could collect money, and build a war chest, without the knowledge of either yourself or Congress."

Kennedy looked a little sick suddenly. "You think that's it? Something so simply transactional?"

"In part, but not at all simple. Start with the failure of the Bay of Pigs, for which the CIA blames you. Yet you still share with the Company, as they like to call themselves, a desire to see Castro gone. And perhaps they are developing a new method to do so."

"How would eliminating Trujillo achieve that?"

"It wouldn't. It might have been merely a sort of rehearsal, with perhaps that side benefit of lucrative work-for-hire for certain oil interests. It would be what you Americans term a dry run."

Kennedy was shaking his head. "No, no, Director Dulles is a family friend. He would never—"

Sand cut in. "Allen Dulles isn't the only person at the CIA, Mr. President. Other people there, who pre-date him in many cases, have the power to make things happen—things can easily occur without the director's knowledge."

The President sat back for a moment, lost in general gloom; then a small smile found its way through. "Which brings us to why I wanted to meet with you, John."

"I'm only confirming thoughts of your own, I take it."

"I surmised much of it," Kennedy admitted, "but you filled in the blanks for me. How would *you* do it?"

"Do what?"

"Kill Castro."

"Oh," Sand said offhandedly, "I would shoot him. Preferably from a distance at a public event. Rooftop, high window, that kind of thing."

"Why?"

"You'd want the whole world to know he was dead."

A slow nod. "And you think that's what the CIA intends to do?"

"That they employed someone of the expensive likes of Glace to take Trujillo out, that's a real possibility."

Kennedy sat lost in thought for a moment; whether the man was formulating a plan or considering how he wanted to present one already developed, Sand didn't bother guessing.

Finally JFK said, "If Castro's assassinated, and we're somehow tied to it, world opinion would turn against us. The Bay of Pigs fiasco was, uh, bad enough—if we take Castro out, even if it's by a rogue element, the United States will lose face globally and I don't know that we could ever get it back. More importantly, Communism would gain a martyr that might become a worldwide rallying point."

A good speech, but it caught Sand a little by surprise. "I don't disagree with any of that, sir. I just don't see what it has to do with me."

Smiling, Kennedy said, "I want you to go to Cuba and look into this. See if the assassination of Castro is indeed brewing. And if you have the opportunity to stop it, uh, please do."

As if he were saying pass the cream and sugar.

"I no longer work in that field, sir, and I already have a job. I believe I made that clear."

"So much the better."

"If I were to say yes, and got caught at it, the U.S. government would have to completely distance itself. You would have to disavow any knowledge of me or my actions."

"Exactly right," Kennedy said.

"I am happy to meet you like this," Sand said. "To share what insights and expertise you may think I can bring to bear. But go into the field for you? I have to say no. I have my wife to consider and, for that matter, her business interests."

Kennedy gestured with a casual open hand. "Consider those interests, then. The Dominican Republic has a new leader already. Once he's settled in, he'll be looking for a cash influx to help right his country. He'll want to sell the oil rights to the highest bidder. In which case I will be happy to put in a good word for Boldt Oil."

"A good word?"

Kennedy smiled. "A good word and a check, John. A sizeable check, thanks to patriotic taxpayers like you and your wife."

Sand said, "You have a gift, Mr. President, for walking the line between blackmail and bribery."

"No blackmail, John. You may refuse my request, and my offer. But I can use your help here, and expertise. Your MI6 craft and your standing as number two at Boldt Oil—beholden to no one on this side of the pond—makes you uniquely suited to my needs. Makes you someone I can trust, John....What was it Edmund Burke said?"

Burke was the eighteenth-century member of the House of Commons who supported the Americans when they revolted against King George the Third.

"'The only thing necessary for the triumph of evil,'" Sand said, "'is for good men to do nothing.'"

"Will you help me?"

What else was there to do?

Sand said, "Yes, Mr. President."

CHAPTER SIX

DESERT SANDS

Departing the RV, Sand nodded to the two Secret Service agents and received barely perceptible nods in return. He walked quickly toward the faux-fort, realizing he'd taken an exceptionally long restroom break, even with a greasy breakfast as an excuse.

A familiar female figure in a blue-and-white floral blouse and navy stretch pants was heading his way, like a gunfighter on a dusty Southwestern street in a showdown. Thankfully, her expression revealed only concern.

When they'd closed the distance, his wife put a hand on his either arm and looked up with a smile. "I was getting worried, John. Are you all right? If you're sick, movie stars be damned, we can—"

Then her expression froze, all but her smile, which was melting. She was looking past him, and he glanced in that direction as well—the two Secret Service agents were now positioned on either side of a burgundy Ford Thunderbird that had pulled up in front of Lawford's trailer, with a third dark-garbed agent in sunglasses opening a rear door for a man in a polo shirt and white slacks and sunglasses.

Only the Thunderbird's tinted windows might call attention to a vehicle that otherwise ensured the Leader of the Free World's ability to travel anonymously out here in the middle of nowhere. And no one would ever know he'd visited his friend Frank Sinatra's movie set in Kanab, other than Sand.

And of course his wife Stacey, who stared agape.

She had stepped to one side to get a better look—as if perhaps this might be a desert mirage—but already the Thunderbird was churning dust on the dirt road.

"That was him, wasn't it?" she said, dumbstruck.

"Him who?"

"Him who!" She pointed at the receding vehicle, chin crinkling. "You know very well *him* who—John Frigging Kennedy."

"I don't believe that's what the 'f' stands for."

She was watching the Thunderbird as, like a cowboy on horseback in an old movie, it disappeared into the proverbial sunset.

"Start talking," she said to him. "Make it good. That was no bad breakfast!"

He shrugged. "I wouldn't call it exemplary."

"This visit to a movie set *wasn't* about showing the little woman a good time, was it? Giving her a little Hollywood thrill?"

"No," he admitted. "Peter came to see me with a message from his brother-in-law, who wanted a favor."

"A favor. From his brother-in-law."

Sand did not want to go into detail; he could not. The best he could do was say, "The kind of favor someone of my ilk is suited to perform."

Her big eyes disappeared into small slits. "The President of the United States, who commands the armed forces and a spy apparatus second to none, requires a retired British agent for a *favor*?"

"Yes."

"To do his dirty work, in other words."

"Would you have had me say no?"

That stopped her.

He sighed. "It's a one-time thing. I tried to wriggle out, but...it appears I am in a unique position to be able to help him. And that's really all I can say."

"And you brought me here under false pretenses, rather than discuss this before the fact?"

"Yes."

As they stood facing each other in the dusty street of a town of trailers, they heard the gates of the fort opening and the murmur of speech. They could glimpse crew members at work moving lights and other gear while a cluster of actors headed their way, his friend Lawford among them.

Sand said, "Can we table this till we're away from here? Even then I won't be able to say much. And I certainly can't share any of this with the KKK, Peter included."

She smiled in spite of herself. "It's Clan with a 'C,' John. I don't believe the KKK would admit Mr. Davis." She drew a breath. "We'll resume this discussion later."

He nodded, relieved to have the cavalry come to his temporary rescue at least.

Or, more accurately, actors garbed as 1870s cavalry, with the appropriate navy blue tunics, yellow kerchiefs, and tan cowboy hats. This included Peter Lawford, Frank Sinatra, and Dean Martin. Trailing after were Joey Bishop (in a kepi-style cap) and Sammy Davis, Jr., in a tattered uniform and crumpled chapeau.

Lawford trotted into the lead, and with a sweeping gesture, announced, "Frank Sinatra, meet John Sand, and be forewarned that this spectacular female is Stacey, his lawful wedded wife."

Sand was about to extend his hand, but Sinatra went to Mrs. Sand first and took both her hands in his.

"Some guys have all the luck," Sinatra said. "Welcome to Little Hollywood, Stacey. The most inaccessible place in the United States, they say."

"I believe them," she said.

Now Sinatra offered his hand to Sand. "So you're the guy who put all those wild ideas in that crazy Brit scribbler's brain."

"Somewhat guilty as charged," Sand admitted with a smile.

For the moment anyway, any irritation Stacey felt toward her husband seemed washed away in a shower of celebrity charisma, as each of the actors greeted her warmly and Sammy even impulsively hugged her and offered to arrange a screen test. The men extended their hands and kidded Sand about being the most famous spy around, which (as Martin said) "can't be good for business."

With the introductions made, Sinatra said, "Johnny, you marvelous people look like you could use a good meal. Go pile in the Lincoln and have Maury haul you to the lodge. See you there."

The lodge turned out to be the Parry Lodge, at the end of the main drag, if a town the size of Kanab could be said to have one. But the hotel was impressive, a big white frame building with one-story wings to the right and left, behind which sprawled cabins and a kidney-shaped pool.

Sand and Stacey waited in a lobby arrayed with framed signed movie star photos and western touches, off of which a coffee shop was doing decent business. Soon the cavalry trouped in, with their blue-eyed leader at the fore; for a town used to movie folk, the check-in clerk and other employees looked no less star-struck.

Sinatra pointed to the stairs and said, "Charge," and everyone, including the Mr. and Mrs. Sand, followed him up to the bar and then off to the left into a small dining room, past a sign on a metal stand announcing *Private*. More movie star photos and western paraphernalia awaited.

Sinatra escorted his guests to a table that would accommodate the whole party—the room was otherwise empty.

"Drinks?" Sinatra said. To Sand, he said, "I know, I know, vodka martini—I read about you. I am a literate so-and-so. Mrs. Sand?"

"Whiskey," she said, "rocks."

"This is a real woman. I know what everyone else takes. Milk for Dino, of course."

And Sinatra went off to order up the libation.

Sand found himself sitting next to Martin.

"So they really call you Dino," Sand said.

"They do," he said smoothly. A smile tickled his lips. "Well, Jerry calls me Dean, but lately I don't see that much of him."

Stacey was seated between her husband and Sammy Davis, who was excitedly telling her about his recent engagement to an actress whose name was not familiar to Sand. Lawford was seated opposite. The cavalry uniforms made for a somewhat surreal gathering.

"Your drinks will be delivered unto you," Sinatra said, settling in next to Lawford. "The Sands, huh? I just can't seem to get away from that place."

Martin said, "Don't mind Frank. He's convinced he's funny."

"So," Sinatra said, "what brings you kids out here in the middle of nowhere to see this bum?" Sinatra jerked a thumb at Lawford.

Could Sinatra really not know that Kennedy had been at the set? Had Peter sneaked his brother-in-law in and out without telling the Chairman? Seemed a trifle risky, as Sinatra clearly considered himself in charge.

"Blame's all mine, I'm afraid," Stacey said, hitting the Texas drawl harder than usual.

"How so?"

"My schedule at Boldt Oil keeps me hoppin'. Today was free and that gave us a chance to touch base with Peter."

Sinatra made a face. "Can't they find anybody ugly to say, 'Fill 'er up?' Hey, I'm a stockholder. I'll put in a good word for you."

The singer was obviously teasing her—no one would mistake Stacey for a gas station attendant; but he might have taken her for an office worker or possibly junior exec.

"As a stockholder I would think you'd know," Stacey said, hardly a hint of accent now. "I'm the CEO. And the company's net value has increased by twenty percent since my father's passing."

For a moment Sinatra sat dumbfounded, and Lawford stifled a laugh.

The singer, studying her now, said, "You're Dutch Boldt's daughter, aren't you?"

"Since the day I was born."

"You know, I met your old man once. At a floating crap game. Lost over two-hundred bucks to him. Hell of a guy."

"He was at that, Frank," Stacey said, the heavier-than-usual accent was back. "May I call you 'Frank'?"

"If you don't we'll have a problem. Ah!"

A waitress in impeccable white right down to her apron and pocket hanky was there to distribute their drinks.

"Whatever you're doing, little lady," Sinatra said to Stacey, "keep it up. Fat dividend checks I like."

Lawford said to Sand, "You know, John, I hope you aren't offended, but I turned down the opportunity to play you."

"Oh, you mean this movie coming up. It's really not *me,* Peter, it's—"

"Yes, I know. But don't burden us with your false modesty. And I only turned it down because I didn't want to commit to a series. They wanted five films."

Martin sipped his Old-Fashioned, and said, "How come they didn't offer me that part?"

Bishop, just arriving, was sitting down next to Sinatra. "They want secret agents loaded for action," the deadpan comic said to Martin, "not just plain loaded."

"Prejudice is a terrible thing," Sammy said.

It went on like that throughout a first-rate steak sandwich lunch, which included a second round of drinks. Sand felt grateful to Peter for encouraging his famous friends to include the couple in their foolishness, which might help take the edge off Stacey's irritation with him.

But he had to wonder how Sinatra, whose volatile streak was apparent despite the good mood, would react to Lawford sneaking JFK in and out of Little Hollywood without taking time out for the Chairman.

You didn't have to be a Hollywood insider to know that Sinatra relished being a crony of the President's.

***

The couple spent an hour on set watching the filming. The director moved things fast—Sinatra made it clear he was up for only a limited number of takes—but the process was nonetheless slow, and not at all glamorous. Sand—and, he suspected, Stacey as well—was almost relieved to be driven back to Vegas by the burly chauffeur, whose presence limited the conversation to talk of their collision with movie star banter and movie set boredom.

But alone together, on the Boldt Oil Cessna 310 heading back to the Lone Star state, no one was listening in. The company pilot, Tom Something, was on the other side of the curtain in headphones.

In the comfy passenger cabin, Stacey said, "All right, John, spill. Exactly *what* favor, requiring your special skills, is the President of these United States asking of you?"

"I can't tell you that."

She leaned forward, inches from his face. "Not good enough, John. If you think you're going to keep secrets from me, you married the wrong woman. I want the truth or you can hire yourself a lawyer when this plane touches down."

The tone of her voice and the look in her eyes told Sand this might not be an idle bluff.

"You're not a lone wolf anymore," she was saying. "There are two of us now. And maybe someday there will three. Or four, or...however many of us there are, I want you alive and well and not dead in a ditch somewhere. Buried in some distant place in an unmarked grave."

He had given up any thoughts of family, of fatherhood, when he signed on with MI6. It had never occurred to him that he might leave the Circus at an age where a traditional marriage, fatherhood included, was a possibility.

Then Stacey had come along.

And hadn't he resisted, when Kennedy tried to press him back into service? But the siren call of who he'd been for so many years—something within him reawakening in the Dominican Republic—had brought that "Yes," to his lips. That and some ridiculous sense of duty. Of right over wrong. Damn that Edmund Burke.

And in the cramped camper, Kennedy had flashed the smile that had been Richard Nixon's downfall, and perhaps Sand's.

"That's settled then," Kennedy had said. "Where will you start?"

"With you, Mr. President."

"Me?"

"I can't dig into this without answers to certain questions only you can provide."

From the pocket of his jacket, Kennedy extracted an H. Upmann Petit Corona, and offered it to Sand.

Accepting the cigar with a nod as the President withdrew one for himself, Sand noted, "Cuban."

"The only good thing about Communist Cuba...and of course cigars like these predate the revolution by a good hundred years."

The President lighted up both Havanas with the big brass lighter, and as the two men puffed them to life, Sand asked, "You're certain your friend Dulles is loyal?"

Kennedy blew a smoke ring, then nodded. "Oh yes."

"Then someone is cutting out the both of you."

"Are you acquainted with Allen?"

Sand shook his head. "You inflate my role at MI6, I'm afraid."

Letting out a small cloud of smoke, Kennedy said, "Well, Allen's a good man. Republican, but solid, a genuine friend, and—more pertinent to our conversation—the Agency's first civilian director. Of course, having joined the OSS in '41, he's been viewed by some insiders as a politician, unqualified to run Intelligence."

Sand nodded. He understood the attitude. "In your

mind, Mr. President, are there any likely candidates who might be part of efforts to outflank you?"

A frown. "We've, uh, lost track of one of our best agents...your old liaison with the Agency, in fact."

Sand frowned. "You can't suspect Phillip Lyman..."

Lyman was perhaps Sand's most trusted friend in the spy game.

"We don't suspect him," Kennedy said. "It's just that all channels of communication are down. We have no idea where Lyman is, but the last time we made contact, months ago, he was in Havana."

"And you think he may be there to assassinate Castro or at least act as some sort of an advance man for Glace."

The President nodded.

Sand asked, "Can you get me into Guantanamo?"

"Easily...but that isn't Havana."

"You get me to Cuba, I can get myself to Havana...and if Lyman's there, I'll find him."

"What do you need?"

"A flight from Florida to Cuba."

Kennedy breathed out Cuban smoke. "We'll have a plane out of Homestead waiting at your convenience."

"Thank you, Mr. President."

Kennedy handed a business-size card to Sand—it had a ten-digit number on it, nothing else.

"My private number, John. If I don't answer it myself, someone authorized will."

Sand nodded, memorized the number, returned the card.

"Thank you, John," the President said. "I know the dangers you'll be facing."

You only think you do, Sand thought.

Lyman, Glace, Castro, the whole bloody Cuban army? They all paled next to breaking a promise to his wife.

***

The pilot had radioed ahead, including special instructions Sand wanted forwarded, and when they landed they were met by Stacey's bodyguard-cum-driver, Cuchillo, who carried a garment bag with a fresh suit for Sand, and another small black canvas bag.

Barely taller than Stacey, the otherwise nameless Cuchillo had been her father's factotum. His long black hair ponytailed back, the somber pockmarked figure might have been an Indian from the frontier movie set. The cut of his black suit didn't reveal the several guns it concealed, nor the myriad knives.

Stacey, seeing what Cuchillo had brought, said to her husband, "You're leaving...now?"

"I am."

Sand and Stacey embraced and kissed long enough to make the bodyguard look away.

Then Stacey said, "Come back alive."

"I promise," Sand said.

"You promised you'd give up playing guns, and look where that's got us." She backed away. "Go. I don't want to give you the satisfaction of seeing me cry."

Sand took the two bags from Cuchillo, giving him a look that said, *Take care of her until I get back.*

The bodyguard's blank mask silently said yes.

She'd said not to look back and he didn't. He climbed onto the plane. In his seat as the pilot pulled up the stairs and shut the door, Sand finally looked through the little rectangular window. Their sleek silver Cadillac was already speeding across the tarmac; with a flash of brake lights near the terminal, it disappeared into darkness.

The pilot asked, "I understand we're going to Miami, sir."

Sand managed a nod, his eyelids suddenly heavy as he realized how long it had been since he last slept. Then he added, "Yes, Tom. Homestead."

"The Air Force base, sir? They won't let us in, will they?"

"Oh, I think they will."

"Well, uh...you have maybe four hours," the pilot said, swallowing his skepticism, "depending on the weather.... But it looks good so far." Under his breath, not so low Sand couldn't hear him, Tom added, "If they don't shoot us down."

Sand was smiling a little as he drifted off.

Then sun was steaming into the cabin, waking him before he even knew he'd fallen asleep. He rubbed his hands over his face, sat up straighter, easing his stiffness. He pressed the button allowing him to speak into the pilot's headset, asking, "How long till we land, Tom?"

"Half an hour tops, Mr. Sand."

"All right. Thanks."

The cabin was small, but Sand managed to extract the clean suit from the garment bag and wiggle into it. Cuchillo had included a toothbrush, an electric razor and some aftershave, so he even had a chance to clean up a bit.

They were granted permission to land away from the day-to-day operations at the base. By the time Tom opened the door and lowered the stairs, Sand felt good. The final item Cuchillo had slipped into the garment bag had been Sand's Walther and its shoulder rig. The weight of that under his arm was reassuring. Carrying the small black bag, he stepped out into the sunshine.

As his feet hit the runway, a Jeep rolled. Stepping out were a brigadier general and a fresh-scrubbed young lieutenant.

The white-haired general said, "Mr. Sand?"

"Yes." He took the general's extended hand and shook it.

"Welcome to Homestead. Brigadier General Ed Keenan."

"Nice to be here, sir."

"We don't get a call from the Commander-in-Chief every day. And civilians rarely visit us."

"I won't be wearing out my welcome, sir," Sand said.

"And your pilot?"

"He'll take off as soon as we're clear."

"Good," General Keenan said. "We have a plane waiting. If you'll join us."

Sand and his bag climbed into the back of the Jeep with the general, the lieutenant taking the front seat. The Boldt Oil plane was already taxiing to take off. Five minutes later, two runways over, the Jeep pulled to a stop in front of an unmarked, nondescript Cessna 182.

Sand said, "Thank you for the assist, Brigadier."

"Safe travels, Mr. Sand. Give my regards to Mr. Castro, should you run into him."

"Not on my dance card, sir, but one never knows."

Sand got out of the Jeep and the young lieutenant was already standing next to the plane.

"I'm your pilot, sir. Lieutenant Winker."

The officer looked too young to have gone to flight school let alone be worthy of such a sensitive mission, but Sand merely nodded and said, "Lead the way, Leftenant."

But the now un-retired secret agent could only hope he wasn't flying with Lieutenant Wanker.

CHAPTER SEVEN
HAVANA HEAT

Making the eight-hundred-thirty kilometer trip from Guantanamo to Havana on his own would be no cake walk. But Sand knew getting help from the Americans would only make things harder—particularly since the President couldn't trust everyone within his ranks. Anyway, the questions, security issues and other assorted troubles would just slow him down.

Lieutenant Winker had proven himself an able pilot and had avoided Cuban airspace, swinging wide to come into Guantanamo from the east. Once they were on the ground, the U.S. Navy provided Sand with facilities to shower and such, and he had changed out of his suit, exchanging it for olive-drab fatigues from his black bag, his pistol and shoulder rig going under the left arm of the loose jacket. He folded the suit as neatly as possible and tucked it into the duffel to remain here until his return. After staining his face and hands, he used spirit gum to give himself a fake black beard, making himself look at least slightly less British and (he hoped) a bit more Cuban.

After snugging on an olive drab fatigue cap, he departed

through a secret passage to avoid the prying eyes of the Dirreción General de Inteligencia. The DGI, Castro's secret police, watched every entrance and exit from Guantanamo, at least the ones they knew about. Organized with the aid of Russia's KGB, the DGI were nasty bastards, and if he could avoid any encounter with them, he would.

Once outside the base, via a tunnel that came out in a barely traversable thicket, Sand made his way to a nearby village where he hot-wired a *cacharro*, a mid-'50s Chevy Bel Air with its familiar tri-colored blue body and chrome accents. Then he drove the forty minutes to Vilorio, south and a little west of Guantanamo where he had a longtime friendly contact.

Frederico Barajas was a Cuban national, but unlike the Communist state he inhabited, Freddie was a capitalist through and through. Key to Sand's needs, Freddie was a pilot with a battered old Cessna that could make the flight to Havana in under the eight hours by car—assuming that crate was still running, and Freddie's entrepreneurial ways had not run him afoul of the Castro regime.

Sand drove carefully, not speeding, taking his time getting to Vilorio. Freddie's place was on the outskirts, with the necessary land to accommodate the plane, and a barn that served as a hangar. He turned into Barajas' yard, then swung back around to the far side of the structure, to park on the grass and put the barn between the Chevy and the road. The car would be here when his mission was done, to get him back to the base.

As he got out of the vehicle, the cold steel of a gun barrel pressed against the back of his neck.

In Spanish, a deep voice said, "What the hell are you doing on my land, soldier?"

Also in Spanish, Sand said, "Freddie, would you allow

an old friend to turn—slowly—and greet you?"

The lack of an answer was as good as getting one.

Sand swiveled carefully. Barajas, looking beyond the fake beard and mustache, finally recognized him.

"Sandy Man, how the frigging goddamn hell are you?" he asked in heavily accented English, lowering the pistol, his grin wide and yellow in his dark face.

"Passably well, Freddie—and you?"

The stubby Barajas had a mustache and goatee scruffier than Sand's fake ones, his black hair swept back and at least as well-oiled as his Cessna's engine. The tan shirt and chinos had been slept in for a week or maybe a month.

Shrugging, Freddie said, "You know me, Sandy Man—just a humble businessman scratching out a living...even if the DGI don't see it that way."

"Giving you a lot of trouble, are they?"

"They been quiet recently. Competitor of mine over in Arego Martinez, he's been using his plane to, ah, import goods from the Dominican Republic. Of late, the DGI has been more interested in him than me."

"How did they happen to find out about him?"

Freddie's shoulders made the kind of elaborate shrug that defined life as a mystery. "Some good citizen may have turned him in. Anonymously." Then: "I hear."

With a nod, Sand asked, "So, if I needed to fly to Havana today, would this be a propitious time, do you think?"

Something rumbled deep in Freddie's chest. "*Habana es muy peligroso, mi amigo.*"

"I've heard Havana *can* be dangerous," Sand admitted, as he withdrew from his wallet three one-hundred-dollar bills, American, which he held up to his host like a chauffeur at an airport displaying a sign.

Freddie's head shake came quick. "*Mas peligroso*

que eso."

"How *much* more dangerous than three hundred dollars?"

Freddie stroked his scruffy beard. "Three times as dangerous, I think. It would be *more* with someone I did not feel such fondness for."

Sand fished out two more hundreds. "Five hundred is a nice number."

"Not so nice as nine. A greedy man, who is not your friend, would ask a thousand. How about I make you a cup of coffee, Sandy, and you be on your way?"

He got out another hundred. "Six, then."

"I thought we were amigos, Sandy."

Shrugging, Sand started stuffing the bills back into his wallet.

"*Esperate!*" Freddie cried, eyes welded to the wallet. "All right, all right, it's half what it should be, but we go back, you and I. You tell anyone about this, I soon be out of business."

"We can't have that," Sand said, extending the bills, but held on when Freddie touched them. "You'll get three bills now, three when you bring me back. Round trip ticket."

"Sí, Sandy, round trip ticket."

The passenger helped the pilot roll the Cessna out of the hangar. The plane wasn't much, but once they were airborne, the trip went smoothly enough, though no speed records were at risk. To avoid radar, Freddie kept just above the treetops, which slowed them down.

The flight took the better part of four hours, Freddie finally setting down in a field a few kilometers outside the capital. From there, Freddie knew a guy, Xavier, who drove them into the city in his 1955 Ford Fairlane.

Barely two years ago, just before Castro's takeover, Sand's last MI6 mission had taken him to Havana—this was his first time back since then. The original heart of the city—La Habana Vieja, Old Havana—seemed little different except for the occasional military vehicle or familiar black sedan of the DGI, and the artwork that celebrated the revolution. The old stone buildings were still the same, though the people looked even scrawnier, more furtive; but the biggest difference was the sounds or, rather, lack of them.

Music had filled the streets when he last traveled these avenues. Buskers on corners, jazz, salsa, and music from other islands had flowed from almost every doorway. Now the city was quiet. Too quiet, as the Rat Pack cavalry anticipating an Indian attack were almost certain to say in their film.

The London of the Blitz came to mind, that time of day when everyone hunkered down, waiting, just waiting for the bombs to come. He had only been a teenage boy, a member of the Home Guard; but the memory remained fresh. That's what Havana felt like today.

Sand directed Xavier to a bar in a backwater area seldom visited by anyone before Castro took over. Given that most of the neighborhood's businesses had been slowly dying then, Sand expected to find a ghost town now; but he had to start somewhere, and these were streets he knew.

Around the corner from a Catholic church, squeezed between two empty storefronts, was a blue door—or more accurately, a door that had once been blue. Now it seemed as faded as the dreams of those Cuban people who'd fought against, or been disappointed by, Castro's *revolución.*

As he hopped from the car, Sand took one last look around, saw no one on the street, then pushed through the paint-blistered blue door. He stopped just inside the dingy bar to give his eyes time to adjust to its dark interior.

Not a ghost town pub, perhaps, but close. An old man was behind the bar, trying to remember how to make drinks; a client across from him, had his head down, not so much sleeping as passed out. Sand moved deeper into the questionable establishment and decided the slumped man at the bar wasn't who he was seeking; he would try elsewhere. Then movement in a back booth caught him—CIA agent Phillip Lyman was lifting a glass of brown liquid to his lips.

With an eye on the passed-out individual on the bar stool, Sand approached the counter, nodded to the thin, white-haired bartender. "*Hola, viejo.*"

The old man returned the nod.

"Two more of what he's having," Sand said in Spanish as he nodded toward Lyman.

The bartender poured two whiskeys from an unlabeled bottle. Sand threw a few pesos on the bar, then picked up the two brimming glasses and strolled to Lyman's booth.

Even more blond than memory served, Lyman's hair now seemed nearly white, bleached by the Caribbean sun perhaps, or maybe just years catching up, the darkly tanned flesh contrasting sharply. His suit was faded yellow, his shirt off-white, his tie loose and dark blue. The seated man had his eyes trained on Sand, who now stood at the booth's lip. Lyman's right hand, under the table, was surely holding a pistol aimed through the wood at Sand.

"Well, hello, John."

"Phillip. How are things?"

"Things are nervous-making, John. How do things stand with you, old friend?"

"I'm a little nervous myself. Might I join you?"

"Please." He indicated the opposite side of the booth. "Slowly, John. Molasses in winter."

"I'm not much for sweets, but I'll comply." He deposited the glasses in the midst of the tabletop, then slid in across from the CIA agent. Lyman's haggard face with its red-rimmed blue eyes indicated how close the CIA agent was to the edge. Maybe Kennedy had been right in implying Lyman had either defected or gone rogue.

"Rumor has it you've retired, John."

"From our mutual business, yes. I have a new career. And a wife."

"So I hear. Congratulations. And yet here you are, decked out in a disguise that would embarrass Sherlock Holmes. You look about as Cuban as I do. Here to kill Castro, are you?"

The frankness of that, the bluntness, shocked even the unshockable Sand. But it didn't show in his response: "Not at the moment. How about you?"

Lyman studied him a while, then said, "No, just the opposite, actually. Doing my best to keep that bearded son of a bitch breathing."

Sand leaned back and lifted his whiskey glass. Lyman's statement was no less surprising than had the man pulled the trigger on that probable gun under the table. Sand sipped, set the drink back down. Should he believe this agent, who had gone (the President said) inexplicably incommunicado?

Finally Lyman asked, "If you're retired, and not here to remove the Prime Minister, why are you dressed like one of his soldiers?"

"I like to fit in. And I needed to go looking for you, and we often came here, so...."

"So you appear to have found me, John. But why the effort?"

"I heard you'd gone off script," Sand said. "Mind if

I smoke?"

He started to reach toward his pocket, but Lyman shook his head. "Have one of mine." With his left hand, he withdrew a pack of cigarettes from a pocket—Pall Malls—and dropped it and a book of matches onto the table.

Sand said, "I prefer *Gauloises.*"

"Rough it."

He shook a smoke out, lit up, took a deep puff. "Thank you, Phillip. Mediocre, but thank you."

"Who sent you? Who told you I went off script?"

"Your boss's boss."

That rocked him a bit, but then he said, "Bullshit, John. How would you know the man?"

"Peter Lawford is a friend."

"If you want to impress me, try John Wayne. Or better, Marilyn Monroe."

"Phillip, must I remind you to whose sister Lawford is married? A meeting was arranged. The man at the top thinks elements of the CIA have their own agenda, and he's hesitant to trust any of you."

Lyman still wasn't buying. "So he turned to a stalwart agent from the Mother Country?"

"Can you blame him? He fears the Company is working behind his back, or at least elements thereof, and that you lot are trying to kill Castro. Which has its appeal, certainly, but would be internationally...awkward."

Lyman let out a long breath of Pall Mall smoke. "We've known each other a long time, John."

"We have."

"You've saved my life, I've saved yours."

"I'm not keeping score, but yes."

"You wouldn't lie to me."

"Certainly I would, given the right circumstances. As

you would to me. But I am not lying and you will have to trust your instincts on that score. I am here because—when I was told by the most powerful man in the world that you had gone rogue—I *knew* it was a load of bollocks."

Lyman twitched a smile. "But it isn't. I *did* go rogue."

With a gun almost certainly pointed at him under the table, Sand weighed his options—and he couldn't come up with any.

Then Lyman brought his hand up and laid his .45 on the table; it was the kind of place where you could do that.

"I went rogue," the spook said, "for the same reason you say *you* were sent here...by Peter Lawford's brother-in-law, no less. Because I, too, felt I couldn't trust anybody at Central Intelligence."

Sand sat forward; a muscle twitched in his jaw. "So, they *are* trying to kill Castro?"

"*Someone* is, someone either on the inside or a trusted asset. So far I don't know for sure exactly who's behind it."

"What are you doing in Havana then?"

Lyman smirked. "As I said, trying to prevent it. I've been following Castro and his entourage. He likes to go out among the people." A sigh. "I thought I was being careful, but somebody must have made me. Two men came looking for me and I managed to slip away. I figured I would grab a drink, a meal somewhere, maybe even couple hours sleep, then pick him up again."

"So we've ruled out two possibilities—it's not you targeting the Beard, and it's not me. Any idea where George Glace is keeping himself?"

That name made him blink. "I do not. You?"

Sand shook his head. "Last time I saw him, he was leading the team that assassinated Trujillo."

Lyman's chin lifted, his gaze coming down. "What the

hell were you doing there, if you're retired?"

"I was there for Boldt Oil. My new employer."

"And while you were there, Trujillo just happened to get himself assassinated?"

"He did," Sand said, and filled the CIA agent in.

Afterward, a somewhat chastened Lyman asked, "So you think Trujillo was a dry run then?"

"Might well have been." Sand stubbed out the Pall Mall. Dreadful.

"What if it wasn't?" Lyman asked, eyes flaring. "What if it's just one piece of a larger plan? Trujillo, Castro, who knows who else might be marked?"

Sand's gut clenched. "You think someone is trying to destabilize the Caribbean?"

Lyman opened a hand. "Maybe. But to what greater end?"

"That I can't answer off the top of my head. First things first—we need, much as I might hate it, to warn that bastard Castro."

"Well, he's sure as hell not going to listen to two running dog capitalists like ourselves. What do you suggest?"

Sand considered that. "The man who sent me needs to contact Castro directly, and tell him what's afoot."

"Would Castro listen to him?"

"I don't know, Phillip. You're the expert in U.S. foreign relations, not some limey agent who's been on the bench a while. But maybe he could go through Khrushchev."

Lyman made a sour face. "What, and admit to the Russians that he can't trust his own intelligence organization?"

Sand shook his head. "We're talking way above both our pay grades," he said. "We should start with letting my employer know that you're *not* a rogue agent—at least in a usual sense."

"That would be helpful. Might help me stay alive."

"Always a plus." Sand thought for a moment. "Do you have any safe way for me to make contact with the White House from Havana?"

"Not anywhere on this island. That's part of why I've been a one-man radio silence."

"Then I have to go back to Guantanamo and get on the radio there."

The sleeping man at the bar stirred, and Lyman's hand went to his .45 and Sand's hand disappeared under the fatigue jacket, ready to ease his Walther out of its holster.

The drunk slid off the stool, wobbled, then staggered to the front door and out into the night. Relaxing, both men turned to each other again.

Lyman said, "I don't see any other way. You go to Guantanamo and pass along what we suspect and how I figure in. Meanwhile, I'll track down Castro, and cling to him like cigar smoke to his whiskers. If he disappears into his headquarters at the Havana Hilton, I'll stake it out till he sticks his puss back out in public again."

Sand nodded. "Keep an eye peeled for Glace. He'll have backup, and I don't have to tell you how dangerous he is."

"I know the prick. I used him once but never again—the only person he *really* works for is himself. Don't worry, John—he won't get past me."

"I'm trusting you in this," Sand said.

Lyman met his eyes. "And I'm trusting you, John. Still, it's not easy, even after knowing you these many years... it's not easy at all."

"Betrayal in our world is common currency," Sand said with a shrug. "But we at least appear to be on the same side of this thing...which means we're each other's best hope."

Sand raised his whiskey.

Lyman responded in kind, the two secret agents clinking glasses, then emptying them.

When Sand stepped outside, night had settled over the city. A cool breeze off the harbour cut the heat of the day, but it was still plenty warm. Xavier's Fairlane was nowhere in sight. Sand strolled along, with the sudden sense that something had gone awry. He walked a block, then two, his shirt sticking sweatily to his spine.

Finally he heard a car turn a corner behind him, and chanced a glance—the car was not Xavier's Chevy, but a black Chrysler. Almost certainly DGI.

With a muttered, "Damn," he tugged the cap down and walked on without picking up his pace.

The car slowed behind him, barely keeping up.

Making himself not hurry, Sand began searching for escape routes where the car could not follow. A door here, another across the street, possibly both locked, with no guaranteed rear escape. He could sprint around the corner... but then what?

The car rolled alongside him; Sand didn't look, just kept walking. He began computing the odds of getting off the island alive if he just shot whoever was in the car.

Finally, the backseat window rolled down. "Sandy, get in the goddamned car—we gotta go."

Sand turned. "Freddie?"

"Sí, get in the car!"

The car paused and Sand climbed in on the front seat rider's side, not liking it. The driver, swarthy with stringy black hair and wearing a DGI uniform, got the car moving before Sand even had the door closed.

"Since when are you with the DGI, Freddie?"

"I'm not. I'm with Victor. Sandy, meet Victor. Victor, Sandy."

The driver glanced over, grunted, held out a hand, not for a shake but a shakedown, fingers rubbing together in the international *gimme* symbol.

From the back, Freddie said, "Victor works for the DGI, but like me, he is a good capitalist."

From his wallet Sand withdrew a hundred and filled the man's palm, but it remained outstretched. Another hundred. Still the hand yearned for fulfillment. After the third hundred, Sand put his wallet back in his pocket, ready to just shoot the driver and take his car.

But Victor's fingers finally closed around the cash, tucked it in a pocket, and the hand moved back to the steering wheel.

Sand asked Freddie, "Where's Xavier?"

"Too dangerous for him, Sandy. He's waiting outside town—we'll meet him."

"What changed?"

Leaning forward between the two men, Freddie said, "The DGI is searching for an unfriendly foreign agent."

"How did they hear about him?"

Holding up his hands, Freddie said, "Not from me!"

Sand wasn't sure he believed Freddie, and didn't know if the agent in question was himself or Lyman. But Phillip would have to watch his own back.

The car snaked through side streets away from the harbour.

Sand asked, "Where are we headed?"

"Victor will get us to Xavier. Xavier will get us to the plane. I will get us back to my farm."

A good plan. He knew Freddie, and had bought Victor, though he wondered if Victor would stay bought. The ride took over twenty minutes, for not a second of which did Sand relax. Then they pulled onto a dirt road and, in a kilometer or so, there was Xavier's Fairlane.

Quickly they got out and switched cars. Victor was already turning around to head back to the city. But Sand didn't relax until Freddie had the plane in the air.

Flying back at night was trickier, and even slower, Freddie keeping the plane below radar, the treetops invisible in the dark. Then came the risk of putting the plane down on a grass field in blackness. But Freddie landed at his farm as if he'd done it a thousand times before, and perhaps he had.

On the ground, Sand paid Freddie off, plus an extra hundred.

Grinning, Freddie said, "That's what I like about you, Sandy—so easy doing business with!"

Back in his stolen *cacharro*, bone-tired, Sand drove to where he'd found the vehicle, and returned it like a rental. He was moving through the thicket, mere steps from the tunnel entrance to Guantanamo, when four men swarmed him.

Cuban army regulars!

Sand felt a sharp blow to the back of his head. He toppled to his knees, then his stomach, vision blurred, and his last thought was of Stacey.

CHAPTER EIGHT
ROOM SERVICE

Even before he opened his eyes, Sand felt the pain at the back of his skull. The mild burn on his cheeks and upper lip told him the fake mustache and beard had been removed while he was unconscious, which judging by his thick foul morning mouth had been a good long while.

Had he been sapped *and* drugged? His left arm was sore at the bicep, as if a needle might have had its way with him.

Oddly, a pillow cushioned his head and he seemed to be on a comfortable mattress. A bed. The ceiling above was green-foam stucco. He sat up. Could this be a hotel room?

Still in his fatigues, Sand moved slowly; he had a blinding headache. He felt dizzy as he walked to an open door that connected with a sizeable sitting area filled with low-slung modern furnishings, overseen by picture windows sharing a corner and looking onto the city. He knew at once where he was—within a towering structure built just two years ago in the downtown district of Vedado, at the top of La Rampa, a street sloping up from the sea.

Not just a hotel room, then, but a suite.

These surroundings boasted money, even opulence, but

spoke also of a contradictory neglect—a patina of dust glowed in sunshine and a certain disarray indicated disrespectful use, furniture at odd angles, empty beer bottles on a coffee table, a wet bar that had been ravaged.

A door proved to open onto a hallway where, in fatigues and beards that required no spirit gum, two expressionless soldiers stood guard. Sand nodded to them but they did not acknowledge him beyond a glower.

Sand returned to the room where he'd woken. He realized he'd been sleeping on a made bed, on top of its pastel spread. The furniture here—dresser, nightstands and so on—also bore a layer of dust. Framed paintings of Cuban seascapes hung askew.

The bedroom connected to a bathroom, and Sand went in and relieved himself. The same dust glaze was here, though the counter by the mirrored wall was clean. Next to the sink was a pink plastic bag bearing black letters: *Havana Hilton Gift Shop*. When he emptied the bag, the contents revealed themselves as a small tube of Ipana toothpaste, a three-quarter size toothbrush, Ban Roll-On deodorant, tube of Prell shampoo, and half a dozen wrapped hotel soaps.

Also on the counter were a stack of towels and wash cloths and another pile that was clearly a change of clothes—clean fatigues. Sand caught his own smile in the mirror—his gracious host had a sense of humor.

What the hell.

He bathed. The attached shower head did not appear to be operational, and filling the tub created some groaning and grinding from the pipes; but the water was suitably warm, as he soaped away the face and hand make-up, and he was tempted to relax in it, then thought better of it. With his Walther M.I.A., he was already more naked than he cared to be, should anyone drop by.

He was in his fresh fatigues when the knock came from the outer suite, rather muffled at this distance and not insistent. Casual. Anybody home?

Must be room service, he thought.

He walked to the door and answered it and Fidel Castro, in fatigues less fresh than Sand's new ones, was standing there bigger than life with a smile nesting in his beard and a cigar at home in his left hand.

"Welcome to the *Hotel Habana Libre*, Señor Sand," his host said.

"Free Havana," Sand said. "A nice sentiment. Won't you come in? *Mi casa es su casa.*"

"*Gracias.*" Castro turned and spoke to someone off to his left. "*Trae el café ahora.*"

Sand led the Prime Minister of the new Cuban government into the suite's expansive sitting area. He took a seat across from a couch where the tall, slim Castro settled in on the middle cushion, resting an ankle on a knee and extending his arms along the back.

"This Conrad Hilton," Castro said, "knows little about real comfort. I apologize for these *espantoso* furnishings."

"One can't be particular," Sand said, "in matters of expropriation."

"I don't know this word."

"Annexation. Confiscation. Stealing?"

Castro chuckled—that word he knew. He took a moment to draw on the long, slender cigar, proving it to be more than a prop. *Jesus,* Sand thought, *was he inhaling?* With the richness of Cuban tobacco, that took rare lungs.

"Thank you for visiting our republic, Señor Sand. I have been most eager to meet you. We share a rare distinction."

"What distinction would that be, Mr. Prime Minister?"

"We have both been woefully misrepresented in the

American press."

Sand laughed, just a little. "We have at that. As it happens, I've wanted to speak to you, as well, Mr. Prime Minister."

"Really? On what subject?"

"Your assassination," Sand said.

That brought a visible frown to the famous features, despite being buried in beard. Before the dictator had formulated a response, a knock came at the door.

"*Adelante!*" Castro said.

A smallish soldier in the usual fatigues brought in a silver tray with chipped china cups and a pot of coffee; sugar bowl and creamer were silver as well, though nothing matched. The soldier served them, both men taking the coffee black.

Sand sipped it, knowing from previous Cuban experience it would be strong as hell; he was not disappointed.

Castro, too casually, said, "You were saying?"

"Regarding your assassination—I wondered if you had any thoughts as to who might be trying to arrange that?"

Castro laughed as if Sand had shared a truly funny joke. "Well, that would be everyone on your side of the political fence, John, probably including yourself....I may call you, John?"

"Please."

But as with Kennedy, Sand did not take a similar liberty.

"John," Castro said, lips amused, eyes deadly serious. "*Are* you among those who would prefer me dead?"

Meeting the man's gaze, Sand said, "I prefer to keep such controversial opinions to myself, Mr. Prime Minister. Now, if you're asking if I'm here to do the job? Exactly the opposite is true."

"You really expect me to believe that you're here to

protect me, John?"

"Whether you believe me or not, the truth is I was sent here by President Kennedy. I frankly did not expect to make contact at so early a stage."

He grinned but the eyes stayed cold. "I am expected to believe that the President of the United States called not upon his own espionage experts, but an *MI6* agent—"

"Former agent," Sand interrupted. "Now married and living in the United States. Which I would imagine you already know from the press you mentioned. And that I hold an executive position with Boldt Oil."

Castro gestured with the cigar in hand, conceding all that. "Let us say, for whatever reason, that your president *has* sent you. To, what...protect me? And why would he do that?"

"Because *he* would take the blame for the actions of others in his government who were acting on their own initiative, without his sanction."

Castro was tall enough to look down at Sand, even with both men seated. "Who specifically does Kennedy believe is trying to kill me?"

"A renegade element in the CIA."

The prime minister shrugged, as if a gardener had warned him about an aphid infestation. "There are always such factions within every government. Without them, there would be no revolutions. But is there an immediate threat?"

"The President believes an assassin is already on your island, Mr. Prime Minister. Possibly with a team, possibly as a most experienced and deadly lone wolf. That he is already tracking you to—"

"Phillip Lyman." He waved the cigar like a wand that could make anything disappear. "Sí, sí, he was seen. My men are seeking him now."

Sand suddenly knew why he was in a suite and not a cell or being interrogated in some grim shack in the woods. *He was being pumped for information.* Violently overt tactics might backfire with the likes of an experienced field agent.

"Bollocks," Sand said.

Castro seemed confused. "I am not familiar with this term."

"Well, the Americans say 'bullshit.' I have no idea what you Cubans say. *La mierda* perhaps. "

Castro's eyes narrowed, and he sat very still.

Silent.

"You already know where Lyman is," Sand said, sitting forward. "You have all along."

The hint of a smile appeared in Castro's beard.

"Somehow you knew I was in country," Sand said, "and....That drunk at the bar! He was shadowing Lyman. He reported that I'd made contact."

Castro inhaled cigar smoke. "The Russians warned me this man Sand was *muy listo*—they seem to be correct. What did you learn from Lyman?"

"Something you may not know, as you only *think* you're ahead of this—and me."

"Talk, then."

"Lyman's *not* the assassin—he's *another* damn protector."

"I should believe this?"

"Well, you *should,* Fidel." To hell with respect. "But whether you do or don't is out of my control. In the spy trade, Lyman is an honorable man—the leper with the most fingers. Yes, I believe him...as far as it goes."

"And you believe someone else is in Havana, assigned the task of ridding the West of a troublesome

Communist tyrant."

"I do indeed. George Glace, a highly skilled and utterly ruthless assassin. Not a CIA agent, but an asset—a valuable, dangerous one. He did the Trujillo job. I believe his next target is sitting before me...but know this: President Kennedy did not order it done. Someone else is behind this. CIA elements, perhaps, but pulling their strings may be someone else whose identity is yet to be determined."

Castro clapped his hands together. "Very good, John, you're almost caught up."

"You...knew all this. Glace included."

"What I know, I know, and others can come to their own conclusions and gather their own information. But this I will share with you—I am not the *only* target."

Sand nodded. "Obviously, Trujillo...but that could have simply been a dry run for you, sir."

"Myself alone?"

Sand had barely considered this aspect talking with Lyman; but the possibility was undeniable. "If someone's trying to cause unrest throughout the Caribbean, who else might be on a hit list?"

Castro's shrug took a while. "My people indicate Silva is the next probable target."

Jose Silva.

"The president of San Ignacio," Sand said.

Castro nodded.

Just under one-hundred kilometers west of Cuba, San Ignacio was yet another of the seemingly countless islands of the Caribbean. Though very much a despot, President Silva was more along the lines of Batista or Trujillo than Castro; but his own man, kowtowing to neither the United States nor the Communists.

Sand said, "With Silva gone, and a simpatico new leader installed, San Ignacio would join Puerto Rico and the Dominican Republic as American interests in this sector of the Caribbean. The United States could squeeze you out of existence."

Raising a warning finger, Castro said, "It can try."

"All due respect, Mr. Prime Minister—it could succeed."

Castro's cigar-in-hand waved that away. "No, no, no. The Russians would intervene."

"Is that what you want?"

Castro looked past Sand out the windows at the capital city he'd conquered. "My countrymen and I did not fight a brutal revolution against the bastard Batista to become the lackey state of Khrushchev. I am *no one's* puppet, Señor Sand."

Now Castro's eyes landed on Sand. Hard.

"I won't have the Russians trampling our land, our streets, and, on this much, your President and I agree. We are an old country become young again. There is no telling how great we can be, if we survive the Russians and the United States bickering over us like greedy children with Cuba a toy each wants to own."

This impassioned speech suggested how it had come to pass that so many of this man's countrymen had turned against Fulgencio Batista's corrupt regime to follow Fidel.

"I've conveyed the President's concerns," Sand said. "That's all I can do."

Castro pointed with the cigar. "You underestimate yourself, Señor Sand. You can stop this."

"No. I'm just delivering a message."

"*I* have a message for you to deliver. To your president. Tell him I recommended that he assign you to prevent the Silva assassination. Or at least to confirm or deny that I am right in my assumptions."

"I am sorry, Mr. Prime Minister, but—"

Castro lurched forward. "Your President cannot trust his people with the job, and no one trusts me. I have done my best to warn Silva, but he *es un imbécil!* He believes I am trying to trick him. Perhaps you can succeed where I have failed."

"How? Is Glace after Silva, as well?"

Castro shook his head. "These CIA madmen have anointed Glace *my* nemesis." The dictator withdrew a picture from a pocket of his fatigues and handed it to Sand. "*This* appears to be the assassin dispatched to remove Presidente Silva."

The photo showed a bland, blond man, wearing a white tropical-weight suit, using a payphone, half-turned from the camera but all too familiar to Sand.

Lenny Warner, a former CIA hitman gone into private practice, tagged "Leonardo" because each assassination was a work of art. A fatal accident needed? Call Leonardo. A suicide to fake? Try Leonardo. Act of God? Find Leonardo. During the Korean War, Sand and Warner had worked together, twice. Just thinking of it made his skin crawl.

Sand asked, "Any idea who he is?"

"I don't have a name," the dictator said.

Should he provide the name? Did Castro already know, and was testing him?

The dictator said, "The photo came through a source on Trinidad, where this individual was seen."

"When?"

"Three days ago."

"How does that make him Silva's potential assassin?"

Castro scratched a bearded cheek. "Your homeland rules Trinidad and Tobago, John. Will that last, do you suppose?"

"Likely not," Sand said. Word had it the two islands intended to declare themselves independent before long.

Castro said, "My friend, someone is playing chess with the islands of the Caribbean for reasons I have yet to fully understand. But Kennedy and his intelligence community are playing checkers and that will not do—not with the end game approaching so quickly."

"Make it clear to *me,* if you would."

The dictator nodded. "I need to protect my country as much as your President needs to protect his. Our source in Trinidad says this man is suspected to be an assassin known as Leonardo. The source overheard this man mentioning he would be in San Ignacio on business soon."

"'Soon' could be a month from now."

"Or today."

"Thin, Mr. Prime Minister. Very thin."

He shrugged. "They have lovely beaches in San Ignacio, and plentiful decadent pleasures you may enjoy, should you need to while the time. Request an expense account."

Castro rose.

So did Sand.

"I'll meet with Kennedy," Sand said, "and make my report. And convey your suggestion."

"In my opinion, Señor Sand—in part based on the popular novels you inspired, I admit—your talents are wasted in a boardroom."

At the door, Castro said, "Remind your president that all of this could have been prevented."

"How so?"

"I believe he's aware an American baseball team scouted me in my youth—I was a fair pitcher. But my curveball was considered not to be of major league quality. Had it not been for that scout, Batista might still be your country's lapdog....My people will convey you to Guantanamo. You may keep the fatigues. Your firearm will be returned."

***

When Sand stepped down from the Cessna 182, Brigadier General Keenan himself was there to greet him. "Did you give my regards to Mr. Castro?"

"It was implied," Sand said.

Unusually, the general took the wheel of the Jeep, which sped off across the runway, heading for a hangar off by itself. The sun was low, the air thick, the heat hanging around like a guest overstaying his welcome. Sand's night of sleep at the *Habana Libre* had been compromised by that blow to the head and a shot of sedative, and the plane ride courtesy of the Cuban military had been bumpier than a Liz Taylor and Dick Burton argument. Sand hoped the Boldt private plane would be waiting in that hangar.

But it wasn't. When the Jeep jerked to a stop—the General probably didn't do much of his own driving in such vehicles—the wide open doors of the hangar revealed a big black Cadillac.

Keenan said, "He's waiting for you, Mr. Sand."

And Sand knew at once who "he" was.

The General pulled the big doors shut, personally, and Sand approached the Cadillac in the barely lighted hangar. The driver's door opened and a Secret Service agent stepped out to wordlessly open the rear right door for Sand. It closed behind him with a business-like *thump.*

The car was even darker than the hangar, but who needed the dome light on to recognize President John F. Kennedy?

"You look surprisingly alert, John."

"Appearances can be deceiving, Mr. President."

Kennedy chuckled politely. "How was your trip?"

"Informative, sir."

Going into debrief mode, leaving out only the extraneous, Sand took the better part of ten minutes to impart everything he had learned from Lyman, and—widening JFK's famous gray-green eyes—the audience with Prime Minister Castro at the former Havana Hilton.

Otherwise, Kennedy sat stone-faced, taking it all in. Finally the President let out a low whistle. "You, uh, had an eventful day and half there, John. You learned more in thirty-six hours than the CIA has given me in twelve months. Your take on Lyman is that he's loyal?"

"Yes, sir."

"And, uh, Castro—you accept his words at face value?"

"I would not go that far, sir. But I've been lied to by the best, and have learned a great deal about the art and can do it myself, pretty proficiently. Phillip Lyman and Fidel Castro are world-class liars who may be telling the truth. At any rate, their stories gibe in indicating the entire Caribbean region has been put into play by someone within your government, or someone paying people within your government. That is to say, Glace and Leonardo are both CIA assets put into motion almost certainly by a person or persons in your domain."

Kennedy said nothing.

"Two high-end assassins," Sand said, "appear to be targeting two Caribbean dictators at more or less the same time. That strongly indicates an effort reaching beyond the shores of both countries."

"Castro might be playing us," Kennedy said. "Trusting him as a source of information may well be folly."

Shifting in the seat slightly, Sand said, "We've both

heard his speeches—how he loves his country, his people, and is doing everything he can for them. History will judge whether that is patriotism or bullshit or a mixture thereof. But I do know Castro dearly loves his dictatorial power. And if President Silva is killed, and Trinidad gains independence from Her Majesty, Russia might well intercede... and Castro would no longer be in charge."

Kennedy's nod was slow. "Have you ever met Jose Silva, in the course of your assorted activities?"

"Or is that sordid activities?" Sand said. "Only briefly at an affair of state. By reputation, Silva appears to be a good man."

"Appearances can be deceiving, as you said. Still, that's my take as well, though his country remains poor. He has natural resources, but no way to exploit them."

"I'm told," Sand said, "that Boldt Oil tried to do business with Silva some years ago, when Stacey's father and Jake Lonestarr ran the company. Silva turned down all offers, from Boldt and everyone else."

Kennedy's smile was slight. "How do you feel about Boldt Oil taking another crack at Jose Silva?"

"With a side dish of finding out who's trying to kill him, and stopping them in the process?"

"Precisely. As president, I can send along a glowing letter of introduction. I do think highly of you, John."

"When can you leave?"

"As early as tomorrow, perhaps. Right now I need sleep. I'll go to Houston, talk to the CEO of Boldt Oil, with whom I at least once had some influence, and see what sort of strategy she recommends. I can fly back here to Homestead then. With any luck I can be to San Ignacio by dark."

"Good," Kennedy said. "Brigadier General Keenan will

have that letter for you. Try not to get yourself killed."

"No promises, sir."

Castro and Kennedy in one day.

And yet the meeting that might prove most harrowing awaited in Houston.

With Mrs. Sand.

CHAPTER NINE
SAND STORM

When she was a child, and her father installed a car phone in his latest Cadillac, Stacey was convinced she had the coolest dad in the world. As she grew older, she came to consider it a frivolous luxury Dutch Boldt rarely used.

Tonight, however, she prized that extravagance, because it had allowed her chauffeur/bodyguard, Cuchillo, to phone and report that he was on his way from the airport with Señor Sand, who was alive and well, if apparently (Cuchillo was quoting) "knackered."

She would have met John herself, but the damned board meeting had run long (her own fault), though that had allowed her to go home, shower, and change into a short slinky black Rudi Gernreich frock with shoulder straps, perfect for a reunion—and reconciliation of sorts—with her husband.

She paced in their expensively rustic living room, eyes on the picture window onto the quarter-mile drive up to the mansion-like ranch house. She sipped her vodka martini (in his honor) and waited for the Caddy headlights to pierce the darkness, and when they did, coming down the blacktop drive, her breath caught.

Finally it had registered, just how scared she'd been at the thought of losing John on this mysterious mission for the President. She had sworn she'd never allow him to put himself in harm's way again, casting her into such a state of frantic anxiety. She prided herself on being strong, and this only made her feel weak. And she hated that.

She'd switched off all the lights, save one dim lamp on a table among the overstuffed burgundy leather chairs and central brown leather sofa on a Native American carpet in front of the fieldstone fireplace, a modest fire going—the windows were open, the night cool for this time of year.

The room felt cozy despite its open-beamed expansiveness and endless parquet floor, a pitcher of those vodka martinis waiting at the wet bar, already half-empty (let the optimists see it as half-full)—so she might be a little tipsy. In honor of the recent Utah trip, Sinatra was on the record player, the *Come Fly With Me* LP, volume up enough that Frank whispered encouragement but did not intrude. The perfect setting, she thought, for a romantic reunion.

She walked briskly into and through a foyer slightly smaller than the tennis court out back. A wide marble staircase gave access to six bedrooms and as many baths, and the chandelier dominating the twenty-foot ceiling probably contained nearly the same amount of crystal as the Waterford warehouse. Her father had been a good man, but—God love him—Dutch Boldt did have his ostentatious side, as many who rose from poverty did.

The door opened and, framed there in his usual black livery, was the impassive, pockmarked Cuchillo, who stepped inside and held the door open for John, who ambled in, lugging a black duffel. Stacey went to her husband, who—of all things—was wearing combat fatigues. John managed a wan smile as she embraced him.

"Thank you, Cuchillo," she said, over her shoulder. "I'll take it from here."

"Yes, ma'am," Cuchillo said, moving past them, toward his quarters at the rear of the house.

They were in each other's arms as she leaned in for a quick welcome-home kiss, then began to run her fingers through that dark hair, coming across a nasty lump on the back of his head.

Startled, concerned, she drew away but remained in his loose grasp. "Where did you get that?"

"Cuba. Ever since the Bay of Pigs, the soldiers there tend to be overzealous."

"So *that's* where he sent you—Cuba. I'm lucky to have you back alive!"

John forced a smile. "An interesting excursion, and it felt longer than it was. Might we have a drink? And I'll tell you all about it."

"No secrets?"

"None. If a man can't trust his wife, he made a poor choice, or possibly she did."

Within moments they were sitting on the sofa with the fire to warm them and martinis to cool them. Stacey's legs were curled up under her.

He raised his glass a little. "Cheers."

"Cheers," she said, and they clinked. "How much did you miss me?"

"Enough to reconsider."

"What, our marriage?"

"No. Never a doubt about that."

"The foolishness of still playing spy?"

He didn't answer that directly. "My mission for the President was, as they say, Top Secret. I was to tell no one.

So I went off and left you...in the lurch."

"I know. I was there."

"So, this time around, I intend to tell you everything. *Now,* if you like."

"Please do."

He raised a cautionary forefinger. "But this will be the only time we can speak of any of it, or anything else that may grow out of it, in this house."

She frowned, not following.

"Darling girl," he said, "there is no 'Top Secret' now. My mission to Cuba is known by any number of people, including the Prime Minister."

She blinked. "Harold Macmillan?"

He smiled. "Not that Prime Minister."

And he shared his trip with her. All of it. From Phillip Lyman to Fidel Castro, and even—at his second meeting with JFK, just hours ago—having been dispatched to prevent the assassination of Presidente Jose Silva of San Ignacio.

She interrupted only once, during the recounting of the Castro conversation: "Did you and your new friend Fidel discuss Boldt possibly acquiring Cuban oil rights?"

With a half-smile, he'd said, "I confess I may have allowed other matters to overwhelm the pursuit of such self-interest. *Mea culpa.*"

Otherwise she'd just sat listening, taking it all in. His voice was business-like in the telling, but warmed up when he concluded, saying, "This is why we can't speak of such things within these walls. Even if I have the house swept for bugs...and I do not refer to termites...and do so on a regular basis, which I will...the dangers are obvious."

"Loose lips sink ships," she said, nodding, slurring just a little, the tipsiness showing for the first time. Of course she had refilled their martini glasses midway through his dissertation.

"We will be expanding our security system," he said. "It's first-rate now, by normal standards. But in the world of espionage, we have to consider every possible point of entry, and this is a big place."

"We can afford it," she said, matter of fact.

"A truly sophisticated alarm system may prove to be a most practical luxury. Darling, I spent a lot of time in the air..."

"Tell me about it."

"*Your* time in the air, while I was gone, was figurative. Mine was literal. So I had a chance to reflect. On how I was seduced back into the spy game by that bloody Kennedy— flattery and patriotism and boredom were all factors..."

"Boredom? Thank you very much!"

He chuckled and kissed her. "Nothing boring about you, Stacey m'love. But someone smart told me today that I was not built for a boardroom. If I have a calling, it is one that draws upon skills of negotiation that require stronger ammunition than words."

Alarmed, she asked, "You're not considering returning to your former line of work full-time, are you?"

"No. But it would appear I may be called upon to exercise those muscles, now and again, and—on a case by case basis—I may consider doing so. That is...with your blessing."

"You're...you're asking a lot, John."

The mild flicker of firelight danced on his strong features.

"I know I am," he said. "It's unconscionable, actually. As I say, I was in the air and going over things—contemplating the dangers I was putting you through. Risking the family of two that we are now, and the larger family we may someday be part of."

"I can't ask you to be someone other than who you are."

His eyes held hers. "And I certainly don't expect you to give up the boardroom. But as for expanding our family, is that where you see us headed, right now? You're a young woman, and your father's company needs your full attention for now."

Her smile was as pursed as a kiss. "And any little Sands would likely wait a while...until the company is where I want it, and you have finally, truly retired from...playing cowboys and Indians. Is that it?"

"It is."

Her shrug was casual, but not really. "I think I could live with that. As long as we are a team—and you don't withhold anything from me."

"Let's seal this merger."

"Let's."

They kissed—the first kiss that was more than just "hello" or "welcome home" since he got back. The kissed some more. Liberties were taken. Frank Sinatra sang, "Let's Get Away from It All."

But when the kissing stopped, she heard herself say, "You know the Dominican Republic and Cuba aren't the *only* places in the Caribbean with oil, John."

Brought back to reality, or at least this corner of it, he said, off-handedly, ready to pursue those liberties where they might wind up, "I'll do better for us in San Ignacio."

"*We'll* do better in San Ignacio. I assume we leave soon. Tomorrow?"

He held up a palm. "'We' don't leave. *I* leave. Stacey, darling, it's just too damned dangerous."

She frowned, more hurt than anything else. "What

happened to we're a team? With me along to work on securing oil rights, your...'cover' is the word, isn't it? Your cover is perfect."

He was shaking his head. "I can't be at all sure what I'm walking into. And with that psychopath Leonardo in the mix now..."

"You're overlooking something. While you're doing your best to save Jose Silva from a world-class, ruthless assassin, you're forgetting that *el Presidente*'s wife, Isabella, is said to be who *really* runs the show."

"And how do you know this?"

"We get *Time* and *Newsweek* in Texas, too, you know. Let's just say a lioness can recognize another lioness. That as a woman, thrust into running one of the biggest of the big oil companies in this great big country of ours, I know all about being underestimated, even after *years* of being who my daddy turned to in matters of business. You *need* me in San Ignacio, John. Isabella will listen to me."

His smile was an irritating, kidding thing. "You don't think my charm will do the trick?"

"You'll have *enough* to do, won't you? And charm only goes so far. A woman like this may not listen to a man, John, but she'll listen to me."

He seemed openly amused now. "Because you're a woman?"

Now she stood. "Don't patronize me! Do you expect me to sit at home worrying while you're off doing God knows what halfway around the world? After I explain to you how I can help you with this, you *dismiss* me?"

He frowned. "You saw in Port Royal the kind of peril I face. I won't put you in that kind of jeopardy. We *are* a team, we *are* equals, but we each have our role, our place."

"Are we talking the boardroom, John? Or the bedroom,

or the kitchen, or just where?"

"Somewhere where I am not. Somewhere where you are safe. Where your man Cuchillo can protect you when I'm not there to do it for you."

"I see. My role is, apparently, to be the helpless little woman, waiting by the lighted lamp by the window. No thank you!"

Holding back tears, not wanting to give him the satisfaction, she stormed out, and up the stairs, and down the long hall into their bedroom. She shut and locked the door, just as his footfalls in the hallway announced pursuit. Then the knob jiggled as he tried it unsuccessfully.

"Goddamn it, Stacey, open the door. This is childish."

Her anger rose so fast and hot that it evaporated the tears. "We agree on that much, John. But not on which of us is behaving like a spoiled brat."

"Don't you understand, woman? I couldn't live with myself if I got you killed."

She spoke her mind to the door. "You're not my father, John, you're my husband, my partner. Don't treat me like a weak woman—I'm CEO of a Fortune 500 company, you chauvinistic British bastard. We're partners or we're nothing. There are plenty of rooms for you here to pick from to sleep in tonight—but you're not welcome in this one."

"Stacey...darling..."

She said, "Tomorrow morning we're either full partners in this corporation or we go our separate ways. I asked for no prenup, so you'll be a very wealthy spy when you get yourself killed. Go to hell or a guest room, and make up your mind."

In the hallway, Sand stood looking at the locked door, knowing that right now he could sooner win an argument with this slab of wood than with his wife. How could he convince her that where he was going—likely to face as cold-blooded an assassin as he'd ever encountered—was no place for a woman?

Impossible, without sounding like...well, like a chauvinistic British bastard.

Shuffling down the stairs in defeat, he found Cuchillo waiting at the bottom. The bodyguard was in a white T-shirt with his black suit pants. "*Está bien*, sir?"

"No, amigo, but I will try again tomorrow. To reason with her."

"She is many things, Miss Boldt...pardon, *Mrs. Sand*. But reasonable is not always high on the list."

The two men stood facing each other. "I have noticed. Could you find me a blanket? I'm going to set up camp in the living room."

Nodding, Cuchillo said, "I will get you one, sir."

That was when they heard Stacey scream.

The stairs were wide enough to accommodate them both as they went up two steps at a time. At the top, Sand paused to tell the bodyguard, "She's got the door locked."

Moving with surprising speed for a man of his bulk, Cuchillo hurtled down the hallway and threw himself at the door at the end of the hall, ripping it off its hinges as he hit it at full speed, left shoulder first. Sand heard the cough of a silenced pistol, and hit the deck, yanking the Walther from the shoulder holster beneath the fatigue jacket as the burly driver went down with a grunt, Stacey screaming her friend's name.

With his back to the wall, Sand eased to the doorway, peered carefully around the jamb and into the unlighted bedroom. Even with moonlight streaming through the creases between curtains, he couldn't make out anyone in there except the fallen Cuchillo, face down on the door he'd crashed through.

Motionless.

And no sign of Stacey.

The big double bed was at right, night stands on either side. The intruder would've had room to crouch on the bed's far side, to pop up for a clean shot at anyone coming through the now doorless door. But if that intruder was holding Stacey down there, how had she known to scream Cuchillo's name?

Not a likely hiding place.

Tucked at the far right, on the same wall as the head-board of the bed, was Stacey's walk-in closet, and the gunman could have shot from there and then slipped inside with his hostage. But if Stacey's would-be savior had taken a hit from that angle, he would not have fallen face down onto the splintered door.

Another hiding place eliminated.

Immediately to the left upon entering would be Stacey's make-up table and mirror, with low-riding drawers to either side—no hiding place for one, let alone two.

Eliminated.

On the left-hand wall was Sand's own closet, unlikely, as it provided no possible escape route, and his armoire, which the shooter could almost use as cover, but wedged into a corner with no easy escape route. At center left, the open door to the unlighted bathroom seemed a good possibility—the shooter could have nailed Cuchillo, mid-room, then quickly dragged Stacey in there.

And that bathroom had a window as a possible point of ingress, if the intruder had brought a ladder to access the second floor. More likely their unwelcome guest had entered the house earlier, probably while Cuchillo was off collecting Sand, and then hidden in the bedroom waiting for an opportunity to pounce.

The entire thought process took Sand about two seconds. Figuring out what to do about an armed intruder, who was obviously a good shot, with a clear view on the bedroom door, holding Sand's wife hostage from good cover, well...that would take a little longer.

Still, knowing where the intruder almost certainly gave Sand an edge.

"Stacey, are you all right?"

"John..." Her voice confirmed her and her captor's position. Then silence. But that one word conveyed many layers—fear, yes, but also concern, and love, and regret, and...all the things he was feeling but pushing down.

He had a job to do, after all.

Then someone else's voice: "Spunky kid, John! You sure married above your station."

And he recognized it.

The voice continued: "You've interfered in something that wasn't your concern, John. I'm not even sure you're being fucking paid. Should have stayed retired, old buddy. Now I have to kill both your ugly ass *and* this pretty wife you don't deserve."

Anger rose within Sand, but he tamped it down. Now was not the time to let a killer as cunning as George Glace goad him into making a mistake.

"Who's paying *you,* Glace? You see these plush surroundings. We can double whatever's on offer."

The assassin's laugh was deep, full-throated. "You know better than that, Sand! A professional who can't be trusted in this business either loses clients or his—"

Before another word was spoken, Sand flung himself into the bedroom, and onto the bed, swinging into position to see Glace in the bathroom doorway, gun arm coming up, the other around Stacey's waist. The two men fired simultaneously, Sand's shot going up and to the left of Glace into the wall, in an effort to avoid hitting Stacey, while Glace's silenced automatic also missed, the bullet landing behind Sand in the headboard.

Sand rolled off onto the far side of the bed. Glace, under fire, was distracted enough that Stacey was able to slip his grasp. She struck out with a sideways kick to the assassin's wrist, sending the gun flying into the bedroom, spinning to a stop near the face-down Cuchillo.

The bodyguard came suddenly alive, grabbing the gun, pointing it upward from his prone position. Sand rose to a knee, and again two shots were fired almost at once, Cuchillo's round entering under Glace's chin and sending a spray of blood and bone and general gore toward where the wall met the ceiling, just as Sand punched a hole in the man's heart. The assassin had barely had time to form a surprised expression before he slumped to the floor in a sprawl of death, half in, half out of the bathroom.

Stacey was already heading toward Cuchillo, still on the floor but on his back now, revealing a blood-stained shoulder on his t-shirt and brilliant red trickling down his arm. After shared nods with his wife, Sand moved to the bathroom, stepped over the corpse, and checked the shower stall, finding it empty. He would need to clear the entire house, and the grounds, to insure Glace hadn't brought back-up along, as in the Dominican Republic.

But first, with a towel for Stacey to staunch the driver's bleeding, Sand went over and knelt next to her, so beautiful sitting there on the floor in that sexy black dress, dappled now by Cuchillo's blood as the driver leaned against her, with Glace's gun still in his hand.

"We can call for a doctor," Sand said to Cuchillo, kneeling, "or take you to the emergency room." To Stacey, he said, "Whatever we do, we should keep in mind we have a dead CIA assassin in our bedroom."

But the driver found a grin. "Amigo of mine fixes things like this, at all hours, and isn't fussy about reporting things."

"A good friend to have," Sand said. "Can he come pick you up and deal with, ah, your scratch?"

Cuchillo barked a laugh. "Oh yes. He is full service. We could probably deal with..." He nodded toward the sprawled face-down Glace, who had no opinion.

"No," Sand said, without further explanation.

Stacey carried her bedside phone over to her wounded friend, the cord just reaching, and dressed his wound as best she could as Cuchillo made the call himself.

When the arrangements had been made, Stacey returned the phone, saying to Cuchillo, "You big lug, I thought you might be dead."

He grinned at her as she knelt again. "I am a great actor, among my other skills."

Sand said to her, "Where did you learn to kick like that? Speaking of skills."

But it was Cuchillo who answered: "From me. Before Mr. Boldt took me on, I was a *federale* in Mexico. He taught her how to shoot, I taught her how to fight."

Stacey said, "Also how to hot-wire a car and pick a lock, among other helpful household hints."

Sand said, "Chauffeur, bodyguard...teacher?"

The Mexican shrugged his good shoulder. "I figured she would be in charge one day. Any skill I have? She has. She would make a fine *federale*."

Sand met his wife's eyes. "You never told me."

"A wife has to maintain a certain aura of mystery, Mr. Sand, otherwise a husband might lose interest."

"Little chance of that."

"Darling—what do we do about this dead man in our bedroom? Don't we have to call the sheriff or something?"

He shook his head. "No. Nor should Cuchillo's friend be further imposed upon."

"So who *do* we call?" she asked.

"I know someone," he said, getting to his feet.

CHAPTER TEN
SANDS AT THE SANDS

—————

The phone call to the President was brief, and however secure the line might be—and one would assume it would be secure indeed—Sand was discreet.

"My homecoming was intruded upon by the individual we discussed," Sand said, mildly surprised Kennedy himself had answered, "regarding possible Caribbean disruption."

"I see."

"Apparently the gentleman decided to drop by and pay his respects. But now he won't leave. I don't think he'll ever leave."

"I will, uh, send help to convince him."

"He won't need convincing. He's made himself at home in our master bedroom and is dead to the world."

"Ah. If he's made a mess, I could, uh, send over a crew from Charon Services."

Charon—in Greek mythology, the son of the night who ferried the deceased over the River Styx in return for a coin left in the mouth of each corpse.

"Please," Sand said.

The familiar voice gave away nothing at all. "I'll take care of the fee."

"When can I expect them?"

"Well before dawn. Your, uh, trip to a warmer clime will have to be postponed for a day or two."

"The clean-up will take that long?"

"Certainly not. I know you've been busy, John, and probably haven't seen the weather reports. Most of the Caribbean is being hit by a tropical storm that will be a hurricane by morning. You'll have to postpone your vacation until Monday, at least. In the meantime, relax, regroup. I'll have the letter I promised delivered. Monday, a direct flight from Houston to your vacation spot should be possible."

"Thank you, sir," Sand said. "You make a most efficient travel agent."

"We, uh, aim to serve."

And protect.

After using the phone downstairs in the kitchen for the call, Sand did a thorough search of the grounds, determining that Glace had come alone. By the time he was done, Cuchillo had been collected by his friend in a beat-up Ford pick-up and Stacey was waiting in the living room with a fresh pitcher of vodka martinis, which they both felt they'd earned.

In what was perhaps an act of defiance, they made love on the couch before the little fire in the big fireplace, Sand confident it would take the cleaning service a while to arrive. To put distance between them and the upstairs unpleasantness, the couple took the guest room downstairs, showering in the bathroom, separately (which was not always the case).

Sand put on a fresh lightweight suit, with company coming; this included the Walther in its shoulder rig.

Stacey had slipped into a metallic silver jumpsuit. On the couch in the living room again, she sat with her eyes downcast. There had been a giddiness following the rescue, in which she'd been as much help to herself as either Sand or Cuchillo.

But now came the melancholy. A human being, however vile, had been killed. In her home. She was dealing with it, yet another martini serving as sedative. Sand, watching from the archway onto the foyer, recalled too well the impact such deaths had once had upon him.

Once.

The doorbell rang, and she reacted.

"I have it," Sand said.

The peephole revealed a fortyish fellow in a gray jumpsuit with several other men gathered behind him.

Walther in his right hand, Sand opened the door with his left. The four men on the stoop wore identical gray jumpsuits, unmarked, like the van they'd arrived in, also gray, parked on the blacktop apron in front.

The leader had short, impeccably cut hair the color of gunmetal, and indeed the color of their garments and for that matter vehicle oddly echoed the silver jumpsuit Sand's wife had just put on. One cleaner carried a mop and bucket, one a carpenter's toolbox, the other a black body bag, folded across his arm like a waiter's oversize napkin. The man in charge carried only a clipboard. All four wore surgical gloves and their jumpsuits had feet in them, like Dr. Denton's; but this was no sleepover.

"Mr. Sand?"

"Yes."

"Good evening. You called for Charon Cleaning."

Not really a question, but Sand answered it anyway: "I did." He put the pistol in its holster and opened the door.

"I'll show you the way."

Stacey was watching from the living room as the little group passed through the foyer with Sand in the lead and went up the wide marble stairs. The host escorted his guests to the room at the end of the upstairs hall, where the splintered door lay just inside the room like a wide plank for a pirate to walk.

The leader said, "We'll take it from here, sir."

"Give me a minute," Sand said. "I've been dealing with my wife. Need a look."

"Certainly."

Tempted as he was to pick up the silenced automatic, Sand let the gun lay. Glace, sprawled on his face, wore black shoes with rubber soles, de rigeur in both the spy and assassin games, black slacks, black turtleneck, black suit coat. Standard wardrobe for his line of work.

The left jacket pocket yielded a set of car keys, probably a rental, which would turn up on a dirt road at the rear of the estate, no doubt. That's where Sand would have left it and then hiked up to the house, to slip in after Cuchillo left, creep upstairs when Stacey's attention was on something else, and Bob's your uncle. Sand held onto the keys. The other jacket pocket was empty. Lefthand pants pocket had a switchblade that Sand also confiscated, the righthand one containing a wad of cash that Sand stuffed away without counting it, except to note that the thick sheaf had hundred dollar bills, front and back.

No wallet, no matchbook, nothing that might be a clue as to who had sent the CIA assassin, although both Sand and his wife seemed to have been targeted, Stacey possibly considered collateral damage. The assassin's car needed to be examined too, but not in the wee hours. Of course, the vehicle likely wouldn't yield any more clues than the killer's corpse. Glace had been, if anything, professional. That didn't make him any less dead.

"Take the room," Sand said to the crew leader, slipping back into the hall.

"We'll be working through the night," the crew leader said. "Could be noisy. Are there accommodations for you downstairs?"

"Yes. Don't be concerned about us. Take your time."

"Thank you. We'll have things good as new by to-morrow."

Leaving the crew to their work, Sand walked back down the marble staircase. He found Stacey in the kitchen, using the wall phone.

"Have the plane fueled up and ready," she was saying. "We'll let you know when we need it."

When she hung up, he said, "That won't be till Monday, soonest. There's a tropical storm in the Caribbean."

"I know," she said, and took his hand and marched him to the guest room. They lay, fully dressed, on the bed of the western-themed room, which had a dude ranch feel, the children of guests often housed here. Neither felt comfortable retiring in sleepwear with those shoemaker's elves doing their work upstairs in the master bedroom.

It was, after all, the kind of night when you didn't know what might happen next.

But for now what came next was conversation, starting with Sand saying, "Being held hostage seems to agree with you."

Her mood had brightened.

"I'm just happy to be getting my way," she said.

"About what?"

"Accompanying you to San Ignacio."

"And who says you are?"

Her smile was cute and confident. "*You* will, if you just think about it. If you hadn't been here, what would have happened to me tonight? Even Cuchillo's presence may not have been enough."

Had Sand not been home, Glace would surely have murdered Stacey, as a warning or message, if nothing else.

She was saying, "Do you really think I'm safer when you're not around? When we're not together?"

He seemed to have more faith in Cuchillo than she did, or at least than she was pretending to. But right now, good as the former *federale* was, the bodyguard was injured, and in this situation—in which the President himself couldn't trust his own people, and with the entire goddamn CIA a possible adversary—Sand knew of only one person on the planet who could properly protect Stacey.

John Sand.

The letter of passage from Kennedy would surely not preclude taking Stacey along to San Ignacio. She was right. She needed to come along.

"By the way," Stacey said, "Frank called while you were upstairs."

"Frank who?"

"Sinatra, silly."

"Frank Sinatra called us? In the middle of the night?"

She leaned on an elbow looking at him. "I don't believe he operates on the same clock as the rest of us. Nor does he stand on ceremony. That's why I was talking to Tom on the phone."

"Your pilot."

"*Our* pilot. I wasn't arranging the San Ignacio trip."

"What were you arranging?"

Now she moved onto her back, elbows winged. "A weekend Vegas getaway. The Chairman of the Board has invited us to be his guests at the Sands tomorrow night. The Rat Pack...that is, *Clan*...are...is? Taking a break from filming, flying into town for one night. They're putting on an impromptu show, and we have tickets. Ringside. Comped."

That was the kind of phone call that could, apparently, make a girl forget about a man being shot and killed in her bedroom.

"And you accepted?" Sand asked, overwhelmed by this little female. "With San Ignacio bearing down on us so quickly?"

Her look told her husband he was the most ridiculous man in the world. "You don't say no to Frank Sinatra!"

"I do, if need be."

On her back again, elbows winged. "Well, you don't need. We're flying to Vegas. As your boss, I insist. Anyway, there's some important friend of his he wants you to meet."

"Who would that be?"

"Someone named Morella, I believe."

He frowned. "Could that have been...Morello?"

"Might."

Anthony Morello—head of the Ceasare Crime Family, one of several notorious Mafioso figures Sinatra was known to be friendly with.

"He's a gangster, Stacey. He's been in the papers. Haven't you read about him?"

"Maybe. I don't know." She seemed a little troubled, on the verge of a lot of disappointment. "Does that mean we shouldn't go?"

"No. No." If anything, it made Sand more interested. "What's the harm?"

It wasn't like the couple didn't already have murderers in their life.

***

The cleaning crew was still at work when Sand and Stacey left for the airport shortly after dawn with a single suitcase and suit bag. As they were about to climb in the silver Cadillac, Cuchillo's friend dropped him off, the bodyguard looking pale but very much himself. Sand filled Cuchillo in about Charon Services, and tasked him with locating the dead assassin's vehicle, then searching and disposing of it.

Three hours later, at McCarran Field, outside baggage claim, a blond young man in chauffeur's livery brandished a *Mr & Mrs. Sand* sign, although no such arrangement had been made.

Wearing a smile on a face on loan from Troy Donahue, the blond boy said, "Mr. and Mrs. Sand, welcome to Las Vegas. I'm Randall, your driver."

Sand said, "Who sent you?"

"Why Mr. Entratter, sir," the blond said, uncomfortable suddenly.

Stacey gave her husband a quick frown, then beamed at their greeter. "Oh, how *is* that ol' reprobate?"

Randall's smile returned, if uneasily. "He sends his best wishes, Mrs. Sand." He took the suitcase and garment bag. "Come with me, please."

Soon they were in the back of a midnight-blue Crown Imperial Ghia limo, its glass partition up, Randall driving them away from the airport.

She whispered, just a little cross: "Why did you snap at that nice young man?"

"A nice young chauffeur picked me up in Kingston, once, unbidden."

"So what?"

"He tried to kill me. How do you know Jack Entratter?"

"Jack's an old crony of my father's. Manager and part

owner of the Sands. Used to run the Copacabana in New York, then Jake Freedman, who built the Sands, brought him out to manage the Copa Room. Jake was Texas oil money, a friendly competitor of my father's. He invited us out here more than once. A few years ago, Jake passed away, and Mr. Entratter is head man at the Sands now."

The fifty-six-foot *Sand's* sign was already in sight on Las Vegas Boulevard. Before long, the limo was pulling up in front of an imposing low-slung building with a rough-hewn marble facade. Randall opened the rear door for Stacey, and Sand got out and made his rudeness up to the boy with a five-dollar tip as a bellman took charge of their bags.

The couple wandered into the crowded lobby, where the rough texture of marble continued with touches of sound-dampening stained cork, copper lighting fixtures mingling with earth tones to create an elegant yet homey atmosphere designed to suggest comfort on arrival and cushion loss on departure.

They had just checked in when a big man about fifty in a sharp dark suit approached, arms outstretched. Six-four and easily seventeen stone, his hair dark on top and snow white on the sides, such an imposing figure might have tensed Sand, if it hadn't been so welcoming.

"Stacey Boldt," the man roared, then swept her up in his arms, making a child of her. When he set her down, her smile was as big as his was.

"Jack, you old rascal!" she said. "How the hell have you been?"

"Spectacular." The friendly face turned grave. "Sweetheart, I'm sorry I couldn't make the funeral."

"The flowers were lovely, and your note...well, it meant a lot. Dad loved you."

The smile returned. "Forgive me, then?"

"Nothing to forgive. Jack Entratter, this is my husband, John Sand."

The two men shook hands. The big man's grip was expectedly firm, but didn't try to prove anything. "John, a pleasure to meet you. You're a lucky man."

Sand glanced around. "A little luck wouldn't hurt in this town."

"It's a goddamn necessity," Entratter admitted, "unless you're the house." With an arm around them both, he walked them away from the check-in counter. "Frank already arranged for your ringside seats tonight, and I have a suite for you, courtesy of the Sands of course."

Sand said, "Will Mr. Morello be joining us in the showroom?"

Entratter's friendly expression froze momentarily. Then, perhaps not as jovial as before, casually glancing around for any eavesdroppers, he said, "Anthony doesn't care much for crowds..."

"He'd seem to be in the wrong town for that."

Entratter's laugh tried a little too hard. "You'd think that, wouldn't you? Really, it's the general public he shies away from. Anywhere the press can get at him. He likes a good social get-together as much as the next fella."

"Does he."

"Funny you should mention it, because he's having a party after Frank's show, and you two are invited."

Sand smiled blandly. "He's one of your partners, isn't he? Along with Lansky and Abrams?"

Stacey clearly didn't know what her husband was talking about, but gave him a look that accused him of yet more rudeness.

Entratter's ease seemed to be dissolving, and he was

obviously cutting the encounter short as he said, "Let's get you folks into your suite. Give you a chance to settle in, maybe grab a swim, before tonight."

The hotel owner escorted them back outside and for a moment Sand thought he and his bride might be shuffled back into a cab and sent from whence they came—mentioning Morello had been bad form, after all, if intentionally so.

But Entratter only waved over a tram driven by a showgirl dressed in a strapless glittery second skin.

"Lee will show you to your room," Entratter said, as a bellman materialized to load their things on.

His smile a bit forced now, Entratter told the young woman, "The Sands are in Room 1001 in the Belmont Park wing."

"Yes, Mr. Entratter," she said. She gestured for them to take the back seat of her glorified golf cart. "It's a pleasure to welcome the Sands to...the Sands."

Everyone smiled a little at that, including Sand, though Entratter had already disappeared, and he might be less in a mood for smiling now, anyway.

The tram ride to the Belmont Park wing was brief, another bellman waiting to convey their luggage as he led them to the suite. Another five-dollar tip later, the couple were alone in a good-sized living room with atomic-age furnishings—white sofa with matching chairs arranged on blue carpeting—that recalled the suite Sand woke up to in Havana a lifetime ago...or was that yesterday?

Stacey stood at glass doors that looked out onto a giant, well-populated swimming pool. Sand slipped up beside her.

She said, "If we were smart, we'd catch some sleep. We hardly had any last night. But I think I've gone past tired into some other state entirely."

"It will catch up with you."

"What was that about back there?"

He played innocent. "What was what about?"

"Jack is a very nice man. You made him uncomfortable. Why did you do that? We're his guests!"

"I'm not so sure we are."

"What do you mean?"

A shrug. "Well, if we're his guests, it's because Sinatra told him to do it. And maybe it wasn't Sinatra."

"John, I told you—he and my father were friends! When Jack found out I was coming, he might very well have decided to comp us."

"I don't think so. It was either Sinatra or Morello."

Her eyes got very wide. "Morello! Why? What was that about Morello and some other people being Jack's partners?"

"Entratter didn't like my mentioning that. They're silent partners. Mafiosi. Your father's nice friend is, I believe the term is, 'mobbed up.'"

"Don't be silly."

"Sorry for speaking out of turn. I don't know what made me think this town was built by gangsters."

She seemed not to be listening anymore. Pointing to the pool, and what looked like a big table supported by pontoons, she said, "John, it's a literal floating crap game! We *have* to try it." She gave him a mocking look. "I'm sure they don't allow gangsters in the pool."

"Not with their guns. Probably."

Stacey got into a yellow bikini and he put on blue trunks and a white terry cloth jacket that went accidentally well with the room's decor. No pocket would accommodate the Walther, but Glace's switchblade tucked away fine. Into the other jacket pocket went Glace's roll of cash, which Sand felt would fittingly underwrite any gambling they might do.

They walked out to the pool, the sun high and hot but the humidity, typically for the town, almost nonexistent. He followed Stacey down the short stairs into the water and savored its coolness; it came only to above his knees, his pockets safely dry.

A few berths were still available at the floating craps table, and he peeled three hundreds off the stack and bought chips. Stacey was ecstatic when they won the first roll, less so when their pile of chips began to shrink.

A perky brunette carrying a tray sidled up to them. "May I get either of you a drink?"

Stacey was thinking, but Sand jumped right in. "Iced tea," he said.

Stacey shrugged and said, "Lemonade for me."

"That's my girl," he said. "No alcohol yet. We have a long day and night ahead."

Her smile turned up at the corners. "Promises, promises."

The waitress hadn't brought the drinks before they'd lost the remainder of their chips. Stacey held out her hand and Sand filled it with more of Glace's money—that would teach the dead bastard. He began peeling off bills, and then stopped cold.

Nestled among the hundreds were ten one-thousand peso notes from San Ignacio.

"What is it, John?"

He gave her a smile as forced as Entratter's, handed her five one-hundred-dollar bills from the dead man's stash, then looked down at the currency from San Ignacio.

Presidente Jose Silva stared back at him from the money. Not likely a coincidence. Of course, Glace might have been in San Ignacio simply to go to the casinos, right? Unlike Cuba, San Ignacio was still a sinner's paradise. Silva did not seem to have been Glace's target—Castro had shown Sand the picture of Lenny Warner, "Leonardo"...right?

The other consideration, far more likely, was that someone on San Ignacio knew Sand was coming and had hired Glace to make sure he never got there. Now Glace was dead, and Sand would be leaving for the island soon. Had someone hired a top-flight professional killer to keep that from happening?

Their drinks arrived. Sipping his iced tea at the floating craps table, he floated an idea—*the person who hired Glace to kill Sand must be the same one who wanted Silva dead.*

Stacey squealed. She smiled at him when he looked up, then she pointed to the table to a huge pile of chips in front of her. They were winning.

At the moment.

CHAPTER ELEVEN
COVER CHARGE

With only a railing and footlights between them and the stage
and its center microphone, Stacey and her husband were
seated beside each other at one of the many long, ban-
quet-style tables in the four-hundred-seat Copa Room.
With the audience jammed together like a White Sale at
Macy's, the atmosphere was nonetheless considerably
more festive—bright red chairs, lime green walls, *bas-relief*
murals of Carnival in Rio masks, musical instruments, and
revelers that purposely recalled the decor of Manhattan's
Copacabana where Jack Entratter had formerly ruled.

Stacey realized that John's eyes seemed to be on her
as much as on the entertainers, his expression conveying
his happiness at basking in hers. But the frivolity on stage,
getting guffaws all around, including her own peals of
laughter, seemed only vaguely to amuse him, never earning
more than a slightly enigmatic smile.

That even included the opening number, when the
leggy Copa Girls in cowboy hats and boots, and not much
sparkly else, came prancing out to set a tone of cheerful
absurdity. Yet John was clearly more interested in her, and

what woman could ask more from a mate?

When the room dimmed, and the stage lights went down completely, Jack Entratter's voice boomed over the sound system: "*The Sands is proud to present this once-in-a- life-time show for tonight only...*"

The on-stage orchestra began a melodic "Put Your Dreams Away."

"*...Mr. Frank Sinatra...and friends!*"

The crowd applauded wildly, but when the lights came up it was Sammy Davis, Jr., at the microphone. The applause continued, mingled with laughter, and, over it, Sammy in the voice of the Kingfish on *Amos 'n' Andy*, said, "Ah mus' be the *'frien's,'* 'cause ah sure ain't the one in charge hyah."

Then the dynamic Sammy did take charge, performing half a dozen numbers, dancing as much as singing, opening with "Something's Gotta Give" and including his big hit "Hey There"; but when the diminutive powerhouse began singing "Witchcraft," Dean Martin semi-staggered out to thunderous applause and cut him off, warning Sammy not to sing any of the leader's songs. After more foolishness, drink-in-hand Martin took the mike, and asked the audience what they were all doing in his room. On his way off-stage, Sammy razzed Dean in Jerry Lewis's voice, getting a huge laugh from the room and Martin himself, who then sang fragments of a bunch of his hits, quipping, "If you wanna hear the whole song, buy the album."

When Sinatra interrupted Martin's rendition of "Amore" over the sound system, then strolled on, it brought down the house, after which the two men fooled around before Martin pretend-stumbled off. Then Frank sang and sang, his voice strong even if (she had to admit) his jokes were weak.

But who cared, when the most famous entertainer in the world was up there giving her a smile and a wink during "I've Got You Under My Skin"? Then suddenly Joey Bishop was rolling out a liquor cart with Peter Lawford following along, smoking, smiling, but looking a little lost, she thought, to be quite honest.

Bishop observed from the sidelines, popping in with a dry remark here and there ("Mr. Sinatra will now speak of some of the good things the Mafia has done"), while Peter's main contribution was playing straight man in a skit with Sinatra playing a parody Indian—shades of Kanab. The finale was Martin, Davis and Sinatra singing a few things together, winding up with "Birth of the Blues." It was all chaotic and silly, but Stacey felt she'd really seen something. That she'd stood on the edge of Right Now and had a really close look.

During a standing ovation that John finally joined, she turned to him and said, "Wasn't that something?"

"Undeniably," he said.

As the audience members were filing out, still laughing, giddy from seeing so much celebrity on one stage, Stacey and John sat taking their time finishing their last round of drinks, the ringside seats now a liability with the whole Copa Room having to clear out. Moving down the crowded center aisle, which instinctively parted for him like the Red Sea for Moses, Jack Entratter in a tux and a smile made his way to them.

Entratter leaned in between them and said, "I hope you kids enjoyed the show."

"Oh yes," Stacey said.

John just smiled and nodded.

A slight bit of tension seemed to be between her husband and their affable host, though for the life of her she couldn't understand why...or maybe she was wrong.

"There's a limo waiting out front," the Sands manager said, still leaned in. "Frank said he'll meet you at the party."

"Where would that be?" John asked.

"A private home."

"Morello's?"

Entratter nodded. The slightest edge came in as he said, "Yes, lovely place. Very unusual. Why, uh...that isn't a problem for you, is it?"

John's smile almost seemed genuine. "Not unless there's a cover charge."

"Oh, no," Entratter said with a smile and a laugh, both of which were similar to her husband's in forced sincerity. "Frank is nothing if not a generous host."

Stacey, a little embarrassed, asked, "Will we see you there?"

"No, I'm sorry," Entratter said. "I'm afraid somebody has to stay and hold down the fort."

Kanab yet again.

"That was a onetime performance tonight," Entratter said, rising to his full impressive height. "Buddy Hackett's our headliner right now, and he has a midnight spot to fill....Let me show you the way to your car."

Stacey made conversation with Entratter while John followed, and then the couple was deposited out front, past the lobby, into the back of what was possibly the same Crown Imperial Ghia that had picked them up at McCarran, though not with the same, if similarly uniformed, chauffeur. This one was older and had some bulk and a rather severe face.

With the glass partition separating them from the driver, guiding the limo away from the Sands, Stacey—more confused than cross—said to her husband, "John, you were damn near rude to Jack again. He's an old friend, and he's been so generous to us. What's going on?"

"Let's just say," John said, "there's always a cover charge."

She didn't respond to that, still caught between irritation and bemusement.

After a while she said, "You didn't seem to enjoy the show very much."

"Oh I did. That Davis is a hell of a performer. Martin's smooth and funny. Sinatra's smooth but not funny."

She couldn't argue with any of that.

"Peter didn't seem to have much to do," she admitted.

"Well, he's only there because Frank likes an easy path to Kennedy. Now Bishop, he seems to be the glue. Five will get you ten, which is not bad odds at all for Vegas, he wrote everybody's 'adlibs.'"

"I only wish you were having better time."

"We had a better time earlier," he reminded her, and they had, in their suite, doing what even second honeymooners were almost required to do, and enjoying it thoroughly.

"I just think it's unfair," she said, "you thinking of Jack as some sort of...gangster."

"He's not a gangster. On the other hand, the chauffeur he provided us with has a gun under his shoulder." John shrugged. "But then so do I."

That ended the small talk for now.

After skirting McCarran, heading east on Hacienda, with the lights of Vegas giving way to desert stars, the Ghia became the obvious leader of a caravan heading out a two-lane road to nowhere, it would seem. Likely everyone had the same destination—the Rat Pack after-party.

Finally the vehicle took a right onto a private drive that led, in around a kilometer half, to a striking house on a small man-made lake. Framed by stubborn palm and mesquite trees, the shape of the structure was round, two gray saucer shapes stacked over a fieldstone base, as if an architectural collaboration between American Indians and Martians.

In a large blacktop apron where half a dozen vehicles had beat them here, the limo dropped the couple under a carport; they were nonetheless among the earlier arrivers, though the party would soon swell as the rest of the caravan arrived. A butler in livery ("He's armed, too," John whispered) greeted them, and they went up half a dozen steps through a fieldstone-walled entry cave into an expansive, rounded living room with modern furnishings, everything white from circular sofa to ceiling, with a view on a swimming pool, the man-made lake apparently not enough.

The partygoers—a sea of sharkskin suits and designer frocks, smoking, drinking, laughing—were being offered hors d'oeuvres and flutes of champagne off trays served by showgirls in glittery dresses that went all the way to the floor but started late, halfway down their bosoms. The *Come Fly With Me* album was playing over built-in hi-fi speakers, the same music as back in their living room not so long ago, though the ambience was considerably different.

They passed on the champagne and noshes and went to the open bar for their respective whiskey on the rocks and vodka martini. After a few sips, caught in the awkwardness of attending a party where they knew not a soul, they were relieved to see a familiar face.

The host, or at least the party who spawned the party, was making his entrance. Rising from the fieldstone cave, Frank Sinatra stepped into the living room, his tuxedo tie loose, top button undone, cigarette dangling in his lips, highball glass in hand. He raised the drink to everyone and got smiles and applause. But no one approached him. You didn't talk to the presidents at Mount Rushmore, even if they seemed almost alive.

The moment he saw them, Sinatra approached, removing the cigarette and replacing it with a grin. "The honeymooners! And I don't mean Ralph and Alice Kramden."

John shook Frank's offered hand—a showgirl had snatched away the singer's empty glass—and said, "Our second honeymoon. But you and Mr. Entratter rolled out the red carpet. Thank you."

"My pleasure, Charley," Frank said, grinning even bigger. Every male appeared to be either "Charley" or "Irving" to him, she'd noticed back at Kanab.

Stacey said, "Yes, we're very grateful. The show was something I'll never forget."

"Keep hitting that Jack Daniel's," Frank said, nodding to her whiskey rocks, "and you may."

"Are Peter and Sammy with you?" she asked, looking around. "Mr. Martin and Bishop?"

"No, no, they're a bunch of lazy bums. They claim to be makin' a movie and need their beauty sleep. Of course, knowing Dino, he's planted himself in his suite in front of the TV watching a western." He moved closer to John. "That friend I'd like you to meet...mind if we do that before it gets really drunk out?"

"Not at all," John said.

They followed Frank to and through a door to the pool area. Along the way they encountered occasional thuggish individuals in suits not as sharp as others in the room. Were these members of the Ceasare crime family, she wondered? They all welcomed Sinatra like an old friend as they passed through, and the singer returned their greetings, without stopping to introduce them to Stacey and John.

The path was also strewn with friendly recognizable faces belonging to the likes of Dinah Shore, Eddie Fisher, and both Mamie Van Doren and Jayne Mansfield, whose combined presence didn't make up for no Marilyn Monroe. With the rest of the Rat Pack absent, this was a decidedly B-list affair—Tony Martin, not Dean Martin; Mel Ferrer, not Jose Ferrer.

Out in the cool evening with a few brave younger guests splashing in the pool—had they brought their own suits?—John said to Frank, conversationally, "This is Fat Tony's place, I take it."

"Yes," Frank said, "but, uh...I wouldn't call him that unless you got a death wish."

Frank had tried to make that sound like a joke.

"I don't particularly," John said. "By any name, this particular rose seems to be doing all right for himself. He's come a long way since Chicago. He wouldn't be the 'friend' you're taking us to see, by any chance?"

Frank stiffened. "Is that a problem, John?"

Not Charley. Not Irving.

"Not at all," John said. "Wouldn't be polite not to thank the host for having us to a 'do' like this."

That seemed to relax Frank.

Floods mounted left and right, and underwater pool lights, created an opening-night atmosphere. At left, a good-sized crowd mingled in the pool area, a few dancing off to one side, the sound system louder out here, Sinatra's voice still ruling the night, "Let's Get Away From It All." The nearby, well-manicured yard lay mostly in darkness.

Then, to the right, in a big canvas cabana, with torches planted on either side like flaming flowers, two of those thuggish individuals in lumpy suits stood guard like eunuchs working for a Shah. They nodded to Sinatra as he led his two guests in, where—in red swimming trunks and an unbuttoned short-sleeved Hawaiian shirt, Anthony Morello held court over several cronies in casual wear and some bikini-sporting apparent showgirls with, yes, the glazed expressions of harem girls dreading being singled out for nightly duty, though for one or two that was probably imminent. They all seemed to be trying to disappear within their rattan sofas and chairs.

By now Stacey's flesh was crawling. She no longer had any trouble understanding John's attitude.

Heavy-set but really not suggesting his despised "Fat Tony" nickname, thick-featured Anthony Morello sported a hairy chest, square jaw, and well-oiled, swept-back dark hair. His dark eyes had much in common with a shark's, though his even, somewhat oversize white teeth with their prominent incisors brought a wolf more to mind.

"Frankie boy," he said grandly, voice gruff, perhaps made that way from yelling at underlings.

The others in the cabana turned toward Sinatra, who might have been a general reporting on a successful battle campaign. A rattan table next to Morello held his drink and an ashtray bore a burning cigar the size of a baby's forearm.

"Tony," Sinatra said, stepping forward, shaking the crime boss's hand vigorously.

"The show went well, Frank?"

Sinatra offered a crooked smile. "We put one over on 'em again, Tony."

"Ha! Sorry I missed it. Crowds ain't my thing, y'know. Now, who do we have here?"

Sinatra beckoned them to come forward, like a conquering general's captives. "Tony, this is John Sand and his lovely wife, Stacey. John, Stacey, this is my pal Tony Morello, a real stand-up guy."

Well, this criminal boss wasn't standing up now, merely holding out a hand for John to shake—a handshake that did not linger. Then to the rest of his court, Morello said, "You boys and girls go get yourself some drinks and enjoy the party. I need some private time with my new friends."

They departed, though Sinatra stayed behind as did a younger, much slimmer version of Morello, obviously a close relative. He seemed to be anticipating a command.

Morello gave him one: "You can bring me that briefcase from my study now, Marco."

"Yes, Tony."

Marco went away, and Morello waved for the couple to sit down on a now abandoned rattan couch. They did, but when Sinatra was about to sit on a nearby chair, the party's real host said, "You're the reason everybody's here, Frank—you go mingle. Freshen your drink, enjoy the clambake. I'll take care of makin' sure the Sands here feel at home."

"Absolutely, Tony," Sinatra responded, reduced from general to foot soldier. He went quickly out.

Morello turned his attention to his guests. "John, I understand you're going to San Ignacio."

The gangster knowing this shocked Stacey, and she realized she probably showed it; but her husband seemed entirely nonplused, saying, "I wasn't aware that was public knowledge."

With a slight, slightly condescending smile, Morello said, "John, leave us not bullshit each other. The CIA only *thinks* they're in the 'intelligence' game. You wanna talk to somebody plugged in *everywhere*, you're lookin' at him.

So, you know that *I* know you're going to San Ignacio, but you should also know I know *why*."

That sentence made Stacey's head spin.

Not her husband's, apparently. He said, "Could be the trip's just part of our second honeymoon."

"No kiddin', taking the little missus along, huh?" Morello said, giving Stacey an appraising look. "Ballsy. But you ain't going for a third or fourth or four-hundredth honeymoon, Johnny boy—you're on your way to make sure that boob Jose Silva don't get his ass assassinated. All so's you can work out a deal for Boldt Oil."

John gave away nothing and, now, neither did she.

"Keepin' Silva alive," Morello went, "is in our common interest. Yeah, and I also know you have a letter of intro-duction from our beloved president..." Sarcasm dripped off those last few words. "...waitin' when you return to Hous-ton. Here's something *you* should know. I been dealin' with Silva for over a decade—I doubt that punk Kennedy has spoke to him more than once or twice, if that."

"Point being?" John asked.

"What I know that wet-behind-the-ears JFK don't is Jose Silva's a cash-only customer. He don't give two shits about Kennedy unless that pup is ready to promise to keep him in power, even if it takes military action to do it."

"After the Bay of Pigs," John said, "that would seem unlikely."

Marco returned and placed a compact leather-encased briefcase on the table next to Morello.

"Thank you, Marco. Leave us."

"Yes, Tony," Marco said, and did.

His attention back on John, Morello said, "So, here's the deal I'm prepared to make with Boldt Oil."

This wasn't the first time someone had ignored Stacey,

the president of the damn company, talking instead to a man in the room who worked for her. This was no different, even if that man was her husband. But she sat quietly, biding her time.

"I will front you the one million dollars," Morello said, quietly confident, "it'll take to get Silva's attention...and in return, all I ask's five percent of the San Ignacio oil rights. In perpetuity, of course."

John shook his head, saying, "Tony...if I may? Tony, you've made a mistake here, and I'd like try to help you out of it, but I'm afraid it's too late."

Morello's fury wrinkled his features to Shar Pei level. "You limey prick, Tony Morello don't *make* fuckin' mistakes."

"I would start with asking you to watch your mouth, in front of my wife...but of course you've already made a far worse mistake."

"What the fuck are you talkin' about?"

"There are three things you might find useful knowing," John said. "First, no one bothered to search me before I entered your grounds."

John unbuttoned his suit coat and revealed the automatic pistol in the shoulder holster.

Morello's eyes were O's now, as was his mouth.

Leaving the jacket unbuttoned, John went on: "Second, if you use foul or threatening language in front of my wife again, you will understand how serious an error was made, *not* having me searched."

Morello swallowed thickly. Indignation and fear mingled on his un-handsome face.

"Finally," John said, "well, I'll let Mrs. Sand discuss that with you herself."

Already on her feet, towering over the mobster, she

said, "I realize, Mr. Morello, that you're something of a relic, so I will give you a certain benefit of the doubt."

He looked up at her as if a stuffed animal had suddenly spoken.

She said, "John is vice president of Boldt Oil."

His expression said, *"So?"*

"But it's *my* company, Tony. Would I make my point better if I were to say, it's my *fucking* company? I run it, and I run it well, and I'm not successful because I make idiotic deals. For example, this deal *you're* offering. You have casinos, prostitution, drugs, and God knows what else operating on San Ignacio. Were Silva to be assassinated, and a Castro-like figure emerge, you would be well and truly screwed, if you will forgive the language."

The mobster's mouth hung open, but no words came out.

"My company," Stacey said, "has at this point invested not a single dollar in San Ignacio. So if we fail to prevent Silva's killing, we lose nothing. Since we are not looking to do illegal business with whomever the next president might be, Silva being gone won't be much if any factor. In any case, there's no guarantee test drilling will confirm oil, so I see no reason to agree to five percent on the terms you suggest."

Morello's eyes traveled to John as if help or possibly sympathy might be on offer there.

"Look at me," she snapped, "when I'm talking to you."

Morello's eyes cut back to her, anger flashing.

"Here's the thing, Tony," she said. "If we protect your investment by saving Silva, you will owe *us*, not the other way round."

The mobster was dumbstruck.

"We should ask for five percent of *your* take in perpetuity, you greedy son of a bitch...but we won't. Here's what we propose."

She picked up the briefcase, hefted it. A million dollars was pretty heavy. She handed the case to John.

"We'll take your million," she said, "and we'll save Silva, after which I don't ever want to see you or hear from you again. Am I clear?"

Morello glared over at John. "You need to control your woman."

John shrugged. "This *is* me controlling her. If she were to get out of control, you'd really have trouble. She might put that cigar out up your backside."

Morello's expression was a Shar Pei's again. "This ain't equitable."

"You're right," she admitted. "Let's amend it—if Silva dies, and we come out of this alive, we'll return your million. Fair enough? Or do you like the prospect of San Ignacio being *your* Cuba, with all your interests quashed?"

His chin was trembling, like a child trying not to cry, not a grown man doing his best not to explode.

Finally: "Deal."

"One last thing, Tony," she said. "If you get the urge to renege...be aware, you're not the only one with access to professional killers."

Again, Morello turned to John, who gave up one last shrug before standing, the briefcase at his side. He leaned toward the mobster.

"Tony, just so you know," John said, as casual as pass the salt, "if anything happens to my wife—even if she gets struck by lightning—there's nowhere you can hide from me. Those things in those books that are supposedly about me? Try to imagine the terrible things I've done that they leave out. Now. Tell me you understand."

"I understand," Morello said, soft but audible.

John nodded. "Thank you for your hospitality."

But when they returned to the hotel, they checked out and John said to Stacey that they'd be taking a room at the Flamingo.

"Wasn't that Bugsy Siegel's hotel?" Stacey asked him, just a little worried.

"Yes," John said, "but he's already dead."

THREE

COME TO VISIT,
SLAY FOREVER

JUNE 1961

CHAPTER TWELVE
DEVIL'S PLAYGROUND

After their plane touched down in Queenstown, the capital of San Ignacio, John and Stacey Sand found themselves in a modest, typically drab Third World airport enlivened only by colorful touristy posters meant, apparently, to contradict what their eyes were seeing. They were again met by an unexpected chauffeur with a sign bearing their name—this time, a big handsome black man with a big handsome black car.

"Welcome to San Ignacio, Mr. and Mrs. Sand," the chauffeur said, with little trace of local accent. "I am Ernest."

The man did seem to be earnest, at that.

"Not Ernesto?" Sand asked somewhat puckishly.

"My mother was American," he said, taking their bags and stowing them in the Lincoln's boot. He flashed a disarming smile. "But I admit, if you were not Americans? I might have been Ernesto."

"One must adapt," Sand admitted.

With an almost military nod, Ernest said, "I will be your driver and guide throughout your visit to our island."

Sand clapped the young man on the shoulder. "Ernest, you're wasted behind the wheel."

"Sir?"

"I'm sure San Ignacio could always use a good diplomat."

Soon they were on their way, the car's air conditioning fighting a futile battle with the humidity that made this island feel even hotter than Las Vegas, despite a lower temperature. The tropical hurricane that had postponed their trip apparently had missed San Ignacio but left behind plenty of moisture in the air.

The limo had no glass partition. Ernest spoke to them in the rearview mirror: "My instructions are to take you directly to the presidential compound. Does that suit you, Mr. Sand?"

"It does, Ernest," Sand said, his wife close to him in the roomy backseat, the briefcase of money between his feet, Kennedy's letter in the inside pocket of his suit coat.

The presidential compound was a huge walled estate on the far east side of Queenstown, as if in its construction Silva had made sure the sunrise would hit his windows before it touched those of any of his citizens. As the limo glided by, it became clear that *el Presidente* obviously intended to let nothing more than sunlight over the ten-foot barrier of massive white-stone bricks with inlaid broken glass riding its upper edge, glinting like nasty diamonds in the sun. The entry's wrought-iron gates were crowned with spikes, armed guards in booths on either side of the blacktop drive.

Are we entering a presidential palace or a prison? Sand wondered, as the gates swung inwardly open.

Half a kilometer down a lane stood the palace, a three-story limestone building with columns, turrets, and many tall windows. A dozen steps led to the spacious entrance, an area so wide rattan furniture had been provided on either side of the double doors for any government workers on break who might want to brave the humid heat. No takers right now.

With a chuckle, Sand pondered the possibility that the rattan furniture in Morello's cabana had been a gift from San Ignacio.

When the vehicle stopped, a green-uniformed soldier stepped up and opened the limo door for the couple, who were welcomed once more by oppressive humidity-drenched heat. Ernest got out and opened the boot for their luggage, but Sand kept charge of his briefcase with its cash contents.

While the soldier who greeted them was a corporal, the slender, medium-sized figure coming down the stairs in dress uniform, with star-bearing epaulets and numerous medals, was no enlisted man. With the white dress cap pulled low, the wearer's face in shadow, the cap's gold braid and gold oak leaves were at first more distinct than their owner.

Extending his hand, offering a perfunctory smile, their host said, "Mr. and Mrs. Sand, welcome to San Ignacio. Allow me to introduce myself..."

"No need, General Barrios," Sand said, sharing a firm handshake.

The black-haired mustached general's smile was less perfunctory now. "Have we met before, Mr. Sand?"

Sand said, "No, but one doesn't learn of San Ignacio without encountering praise for Presidente Silva's chief military officer."

And, Sand knew, *head of security.*

The general half-bowed. "Mr. Sand, you do me honor."

Then, turning to Stacey, he said, "We will endeavor to help you enjoy your stay, Mrs. Sand."

Stacey extended her arm for the handshake ritual, but the military man took only her fingertips and kissed them.

Stacey just smiled, and so did Sand. Old World elegance always played well with these Texas girls.

"You will find San Ignacio a tropical paradise," Barrios said, "but a paradise with a clime often more representative of a devil's playground. Shall we go inside and leave this heat to itself?"

Sand said, "An excellent suggestion."

The three climbed the stairs to the shaded portico, Ernest and the soldier remaining near the Lincoln; Sand, of course, hung onto the briefcase.

The general led them into the palace through the white marble-floored entryway, with white marble stairs to the second floor on either side, soldiers and office workers going up and down—not scurrying exactly, but not tarrying either. An atrium let in plenty of sunlight through which workers took short cuts. Barrios led the Sands to a corner of the foyer where there was no foot traffic.

When they had some semblance of privacy, the general said, "I'm sorry, but your meeting with President Silva has been postponed indefinitely."

Sand's radar kicked up a notch, but he gave away nothing. Next to him, Stacey remained as impassive as if Barrios had just informed them the sky was blue.

"That's unfortunate," Sand said. "We've come a distance."

"There is no helping it," Barrios said. "President Silva has fallen ill. He has, in fact, been bedridden for nearly a month now, and I must remind you that this trip was not initiated through our offices."

"Has *el Presidente* received any visitors during his illness?"

"He had been doing so, yes, but Señora Silva has prevailed upon her husband to follow his physician's dictates strictly. You see, President Silva has an important speech in two days. It's vital he make this address, so complete rest is imperative."

Stacey said, "We understood that President Kennedy himself conveyed our request. Meaning no offense, why was our visit approved if seeing Presidente Silva was impossible?"

Barrios lowered his head, smiling respectfully. "Our meeting with you is important to San Ignacio. We hoped *el Presidente* might have recovered enough to...but no. Tomorrow, Señora Silva herself will sit down with you both. I will be present. We have President Silva's full confidence, so it will be, how do you say...*equivalente?* My English, I'm afraid, is at best serviceable."

Barrios's English was, Sand felt, better than most Americans.

"Equivalent," Sand said.

"Yes. Two words nearly the same and yet I stumble. Meeting with Señora Silva will be much the same as meeting with Presidente Silva himself...and the best we can offer under the circumstances."

Stacey's smile seemed to indicate she was buying the general's...how do you say bollocks in Spanish? *La mierda* would do. But Sand knew she was no more convinced than he was.

"Tonight," the general was saying, "Señora Silva hopes to make it up to you. She is hosting a dinner in your honor at the premier supper club in Queenstown— *La Perla De La Noche.*"

"The Pearl of the Night," Stacey said. "How lovely."

"You will see just how lovely," Barrios said, beaming somewhat obsequiously. "You will be our guests. In the meantime, we have reserved a private cottage here within the compound for your stay."

Sand said, "Very generous, General."

"Your luggage is already being transported. You will find conveyance waiting just outside."

Stacey said, "Please tell Señora Silva how grateful we are to receive such a gracious welcome."

Another half-bow. "We hope to make a good impression on our new friends, Mrs. Sand. May we say, dinner at eight?"

"You may," she said with a nod.

"Then, if you will excuse me, I will inform Mrs. Silva that you will honor us."

"Please," Sand said.

The general left them, and they wandered back onto the portico. At the bottom of the stairs, a golf cart waited, a crisply uniformed soldier behind the wheel. Within the walls of the vast palace compound, a path wide enough only for strolling or riding in a cart angled through lush jungle gardens to a clearing, where they were dropped off and directed to one of half a dozen scattered white stucco mini-bungalows with faded red-tile roofs sharing a blacktop apron and lane.

A key was waiting in the door. When they went inside, their bags were there. The interior was cozy, the living room furnished with more rattan and the walls bearing framed seascapes not worthy of theft.

When Stacey began to speak, Sand held a finger to his lips, then began a sweep of the place for listening devices. He found the bathroom was clean—free of bugs, living or electronic—but discovered wired mini-mics in the living room, the small bedroom, in lamps mostly. The tiny space that passed for a kitchen was free of them.

While he was at it, he took some newspaper and removed the packets of money from the briefcase; he wrapped the packets of cash and stowed them in the fridge's freezer.

They had a small private swimming pool out back, where the only bugs were of a kind you just had to put up with. He considered whether the little kitchen and/or the pool might be safe for conversation. But the former might have something built-in he hadn't spotted, and the pool might be prey from microphones in nearby foliage. Still, he did not remove any of the button mics from lamps.

Once he'd made his inventory, Sand gave Stacey a silent tour, pointing them out. Then in front of a living room lamp, he asked her, "Fancy a shower before dinner?"

As he emphatically nodded, indicating what her response should be, she said, "Sure. But a cold one, please, in this heat."

"Agreed."

Once they were naked under the cold spray, he said, quietly, "Something's not right."

"I gathered," she said. "Could Silva be dead? Killed before we even got here?"

"Hard to say. But he's certainly not going to be giving a vital speech to San Ignacio from beyond."

Water ran down her face like tears. "Not without a Ouija board, he isn't."

"If Leonardo's already struck, why conceal it? If an illness has taken Silva out...again, what's the point of hiding it? And what have they done with the body?"

"If he *is* dead, does it matter?"

"Well, it would to him," Sand said dryly, despite the

drilling water.

"Not to us," Stacey said, as cold as the nozzle's spatter. "We could strike a deal with Señora Silva just as easily as with Silva himself, couldn't we?"

"Possibly. If Silva was murdered, however, or simply passed away, we may have arrived at an inconvenient time—with Señora Silva and Barrios trying to decide what the hell to do about, and *with*, a dead presidente."

"If he's alive, where *is* he?" Absent-mindedly, she began to soap herself. Sand watched and tried to maintain his focus.

Then he took the soap from her, and soaped up himself as he said, "Barrios didn't say anything about a hospital. So I'm thinking, if Silva's really ill, he's likely in the palace, or at least somewhere on these grounds. His bedroom or an in-house infirmary or perhaps one of these cottages, being attended to."

"Makes sense," she said.

"The thing is, there isn't time before dinner for me to go looking for him, and that's better done after dark anyway. Later perhaps I could go for a moonlight stroll."

"Hey, I'm getting chills. I'm goosebumps all over."

"I noticed." Hair dripping, he dipped down and kissed a breast. "Rock hard," he said approvingly of her nipple.

"You too," she said, her hand appraising the situation.

"This isn't," he said, "how cold showers are supposed to work."

He twisted the HOT dial.

"Well that's just tepid," he said after a while.

"We can make our own steam," she said.

"Brilliant suggestion. With the bedroom bugged, let's entertain ourselves, not the eavesdroppers."

They did.

***

Dressed for dinner–him in his Saville Row-tailored black tuxedo and her in a clingy gold Givenchy gown—Sand phoned the palace switchboard to inquire about a ride, and was told to look outside. He did, and they found Ernest waiting with the Lincoln. Upon seeing them, the driver opened the rear door and gestured with an open hand.

"If I may say," Ernest said, under a starry tropical sky, the sultry evening touched with ocean coolness, "you make a lovely couple indeed."

Neither of the Sands chose to argue with that assessment.

The chauffeur drove them to a busy part of the city, where clubs and casinos wore garish neon like costume jewelry, the night lit up like gaudy day. The tasteless, unabashed come-on of it all gave Vegas a run for the money—*anyone's* money.

Ernest pulled up to *La Perla De La Noche* and a figure almost as elaborately uniformed as General Barrios opened the rear door and helped Stacey out.

As Sand came around the vehicle, Ernest nodded across the way and said, "I'll be close by, sir, should you need me."

Sand thanked him, tipped the uniformed attendant, and—as the Lincoln drew away—the couple moved gracefully, arm in arm, toward the double-door entry. Sand worked an oversize faux-pearl knob, pushed the slab open, releasing smoke and Latin music in equal measures.

Stacey said, "Just another quiet night in the Tropics."

Sand nodded, though it was already hard to hear her over the brassy Xavier Cugat-style orchestra and the voices of merrymakers...and they were barely inside.

The club seemed surprisingly well-lit—as were many of its patrons, *not* surprisingly—and the pastels and Rio-style decor recalled almost eerily that of the Copa Room. The place was crowded as hell and damn near as hot, the air conditioning doing its best, which wasn't nearly good enough, cigarette and cigar smoke floating in thick clouds, as if firemen with axes might rush in any moment. The raucous noise had everyone screaming to be heard over the blare of music—"El Marijuano" going right now.

At a lectern, a short Latin with slicked back hair, a serviceable tuxedo, and a Cesar Romero mustache smiled as the couple approached.

Before Sand could even speak, the maître d' said, "Ah, *Señor y Señora Sand—bienvenidos!*"

The little man had perfected making shouting sound like normal speech.

He was saying, "Welcome to *La Perla De La Noche!*"

Sand smiled, nodded, barely. Stacey was looking at the little man as if he might be psychic.

"If you will just follow me," he said, leaving his post and waving vaguely ahead of himself, "your table is prepared for you and your party."

But he led them not into the massive dining room with its dance floor, orchestra and stage, rather moving them past the seemingly endless bar and down a short hallway to an old-fashioned elevator with a steel grate, which was drawn back by an ancient boy within, sitting on a bar stool.

Once they were all inside, the maître d' said to the operator, "*La caja del presidente.*"

Both Sand and Stacey were conversant enough in Spanish to translate that into "the Presidential box." As the elevator went up, the downstairs noise went down, but only slightly. Then the grate parted onto an open box above the dining room and its dance floor, overlooking the stage.

The area held three rectangular tables, each with six

chairs, a small San Ignacio flag serving as centerpiece on each one, with name cards at place settings. The tables were arranged at right angles so that the diners on either side could clearly see the action below—another odd echo of the Copa room.

The maître d' yanked out a chair at the center table, the seat nearest the stage, and said, "Señora Sand, you are here, please...and Señor Sand, if you would, you are across from her. I am sure the rest of your party will be along directly."

A pretty waitress in a rainbow dress materialized to take their drink orders. Then the elevator disgorged the grandly uniformed General Barrios with a beautiful, curvaceous Latina on his arm, her ebony hair piled high, her low-cut black-and-silver gown revealing ample, admirable cleavage. Following was a six-man uniformed security team.

Unless that elevator had the capacity of a circus clown car, Sand figured the security contingent had used the stairs. He rose and pulled out the chair next to him, aware the name card next to his said ISABELLA SILVA. Across the table, General Barrios made his usual half-bow to Stacey before standing behind the seat next to her.

The six guards assembled at the two tables that book-ended the center main one.

Barrios said, "Mr. and Mrs. Sand, may I introduce Señora Isabella Silva, First Lady of San Ignacio."

Also still on his feet, Sand smiled and gave his own half-bow, the First Lady's almond-shaped brown eyes dancing as she appraised him as if he were a new item just added onto a too-familiar menu. He kissed her hand and the small perfect white teeth formed a big smile.

Barrios had no corner on the Old World elegance market.

"Señor Sand, how *galante*," Isabella said, returning the

bow, and providing an even better look at her impressive upper carriage. "I have looked forward to meeting you. I have enjoyed your adventures—the Spanish translations are quite excellent."

"In any language," Sand said, "those are somewhat embarrassing exaggerations. I am afraid I am doomed to disappoint."

General Barrios, sounding a little strained, said, "And this, Señora First Lady, is Mrs. Sand."

"Call me Stacey," she said, extending her hand across the table.

Isabella barely glanced at her as she dutifully took the hand. "Welcome to San Ignacio, Stacey." Then the First Lady glanced back at Sand, poised behind her chair. "Such gentlemen in our sorry modern world are now rare," she commented, taking her seat with his aid.

Sand sat, smiled politely. "A pleasure and honor to meet you, Señora Silva."

"Isabella. Please."

"Isabella," he said. He tasted the word like wine he was checking for a waiter, and approving it. "And I'm John."

"First names," she said in her heavily accented way, "put new friendships on a faster course, don't you think?"

He glanced across at Stacey—who was doing a good job at hiding her irritation with the diva—and said, "We were sorry to hear that President Silva has taken ill."

Isabella gave a little shrug. "*Es una cosa pequeña.* He is getting stronger by the day. But even great men must suffer life's little indignities, yes?"

"Not to mention the big ones," Sand said.

Leaning in to be heard over the orchestra playing "Malagueña Salerosa," Barrios said, "President Silva is a fighter, a soldier. Where better for him to fight such indignities than on San Ignacio? After all, this island is named for the patron saint of soldiers. If a soldier cannot find solace here, he cannot find it anywhere."

Sand didn't visibly react when Isabella rested a gentle hand on his thigh under the table.

She was saying, "He's right, you know. *Es muy tranquillo* here. You come for a short visit, but in the end you wish to stay forever." Her eyes were on his, as if his wife were not seated across the table, all the more significant because the First Lady was rubbing his thigh like she hoped he might grant her three wishes. Or maybe just one.

The small talk kept up, as did the mild flirtation above and the serious temptation below. Dinner was delicious, particularly the marinated skirt steak with Chimichurri sauce, and the orchestra's songbird was doing a fair impression of Abbe Lane, visually and aurally. As they waited for the Flan de Coco dessert, Isabella—perhaps since Stacey's annoyance was starting to show—finally took a break from dalliance to talk to Stacey about the oil business.

The business talk was so preliminary, so basic, Sand paid little attention, watching the singer doing sexy rhumba moves. A thin blond man in a charcoal suit, seated against the far wall past the dance floor, was enjoying the show, too. The smoky room made identification difficult, yet even so, Sand knew Lenny Warner when he saw him.

This was Leonardo, all right.

The assassin said to be targeting President Silva just happened to be in the same San Ignacio night club that he was? Sand didn't think so.

Interrupting, he said to Stacey, accompanied by a hard-eyed look that didn't go with his smile, "That singer is a real work of art."

Stacey's eyes widened enough to tell him she got his meaning. She had never seen Leonardo herself, but her husband had filled her in on every particular.

Sand let a few moments pass before he stood, excused himself, and left the table, which caused two security officers to half-stand before Barrios motioned them to sit.

Forgoing the elevator and its ancient attendant, Sand ran down the narrow staircase to the main floor, and squeezed through the revelers at the edge of the dance floor; but when he got a view on where Leonardo had been seated, the chair was empty, the killer gone.

"Damn," Sand muttered, eyes scanning swiftly the tables, the dance floor—no Leonardo. He turned to see, coming out of a restroom near the front, the assassin straightening his tie. In a nondescript suit, his blond hair oiled and parted, Leonardo stood out only because he didn't have the look of either a tourist or a local. His very face-in-the-crowd persona did not serve him well here....

Sand started toward the man, hoping to God that Leonardo would not turn and see him. But that was exactly what the assassin did; whether out of a lifetime of training or just from living in a world where you had to be on guard every second, Lenny Warner looked back and his eyes locked with Sand's.

And then Leonardo was gone, cutting through the crowd and out the front door, bumping into some newcomers and startling the doorman.

Sand pushed past two laughing couples, then was slowed like a salmon swimming upstream by a mass of people who uttered condemnation in Spanish, only some of which he understood, though their nasty looks spoke a universal language. But finally, he was past the crowd and outside.

He looked left—sidewalks thronged with tourists and locals, but that face-in-the-crowd in a charcoal suit did not stand out. He looked right—same damned thing!

Sand's eyes next landed on the black Lincoln parked across the street, Ernest behind the wheel, side window rolled down as the driver enjoyed a cigarette. Their eyes met, and the chauffeur looked back over his shoulder as if he were checking traffic behind him, and jerked his thumb in that direction.

Sand took off to the right, sometimes running on the sidewalk, sometimes in the street, as pedestrians allowed. When he got to an alley that bisected the block, where the bars and the patrons they attracted were thinning, there the assassin was, a good block ahead already, walking fast. Taking pursuit, Sand narrowed the distance but Leonardo peeked over his shoulder and knew he'd been made. The assassin's fast walking turned into a sprint, and Sand ran flat out, managing not to slow down as he yanked the Walther from under his left shoulder.

And then both men were running full bore.

The night was sucking sweat from Sand's pores, his lungs burning, but he pushed himself, narrowing the distance as the nightclub district receded behind them.

A car behind Sand accelerated—he glanced back at a big dark sedan, its headlights off, bearing down on him like a panther on a tapir.

The predator had become the prey!

Did Warner have an accomplice? Pro assassins often worked with advance scouts, and hadn't Glace utilized an entire back-up team?

With no major options till the next corner, Sand began looking for a doorway or a low-hanging fire escape—no help. When his focus returned to Leonardo's direction, the bastard had disappeared! Despite that car behind him, Sand slowed somewhat. Had Leonardo made the next intersection, an alley, having run to either the left or right? Or had the killer lagged to lay in wait, in ambush...and if so, on which side?

Sand considered stopping, spinning, and shooting the driver of the car bearing down; but if his pursuer turned on the headlights, Sand would be blinded, getting run down before he could get off a clean shot.

He pressed forward.

Then, up ahead not far, Leonardo leapt from around the corner of the building on the right, and Sand dove left as the assassin's silenced pistol coughed once, twice. The bullets ripped the brick wall above him. Sand's return round missed, kicking brick dust to one side of Leonardo's head. That stopped the killer for half a second, during which time the pursuing car slammed to a halt, switching on its high beams, blinding Leonardo.

But before Sand could squeeze off another round, Leonardo tucked around the corner.

Ernest, through his open car window, said, "Mr. Sand, are you all right?"

Brushing off the dirt, his tux torn, Sand said sarcastically, "Tickety boo." Then he changed his tone: "Thank you, Ernest. You rolled up at just the right time."

The chauffeur got out of the car and handed Sand a whisk broom. As Sand utilized it, Ernest said, "Looked as though you might need a hand."

"Ernest, you may well have saved my life."

Opening the car's back door, the chauffeur said, "I haven't lost a passenger yet, sir. Back to the Pearl?"

"Back to the Pearl."

Settling into the backseat, Sand took satisfaction only in

two things, beyond still being alive: that he had confirmed the threat on Silva's life was genuine.

And that the assassin was indeed Leonardo, a world-class killer who—on a less happy note—did not know that what stood between him and his target was John Sand.

CHAPTER THIRTEEN

SILVA LINING

On his return to *La Perla De La Noche*, **Sand learned that Mrs.** Sand had left with Señora Silva and General Barrios not long before.

"Señora Silva said she needed to get back to the palace," the maître d' told him. "I believe your wife also returned to your quarters at the royal compound."

Soon the chauffeur was pulling the black Lincoln up in front of the guest cottage, with Sand saying, "I'll let myself out. Thank you again, Ernest."

When Sand paused and dug in his pocket for the remainder of the Glace bankroll, peeling off a few bills, Ernest noted this in the rear view mirror and turned, shaking his head.

"Please, sir. No gratuity is necessary or desired. If I have done good for you, I ask only that you do good for San Ignacio."

As the limo pulled off, Sand thought, smiling, *Yes, they really should make a diplomat out of that man....*

Stacey, still in the Givenchy gown, was curled up on the bed atop its nubby spread, a glass of whiskey (sans rocks) on the rattan nightstand.

Resting but not asleep, she rolled over, sat up, and assessed the sorry state of her husband's tuxedo and his generally mussed-up self. Her mouth dropped open, eager to deliver a question; but he held up a palm and stopped her.

He nodded toward the bugged lamp on the nightstand by her whiskey. "What would you say to a swim under the stars, darling?"

"Sounds romantic," she said, as if it really did right now.

Sand went outside and checked the undergrowth near the cottage for any spyware, then returned to the bedroom and got into his bathing trunks. Stacey was already in her white bikini making its nice contrast with her supple tanned flesh; she snugged on a white bathing cap.

The pool was small, its depth five-feet or so; unheated, but why would it be, here in the Tropics? In fact, getting in felt rather cold, refreshingly so, if not as bracing as that shower earlier had been.

They treaded water as they talked, the night still but for the chirps, croaks and cries of nocturnal birds, the sky suitably starry and a nearly full moon touching everything with its ivory fingers.

"Voices low," he advised.

"That was Leonardo, wasn't it?" she asked, her eyes intense. "Across the dance floor?"

"Yes," he said, and told her all of it, the exchange of gunfire and Ernest's intervention included.

By the end of his narrative, the treading had ceased and they were standing, the pool just deep enough that only Stacey's head was above water, and it took her tip-toes to manage that.

Then they embraced. She hugged him close, holding on to him with a kind of desperation. He led her, trudging through the cool water, to the poolside where they sat with their legs in the water. She was kicking just a little, and there was something wonderfully child-like about it that endeared her to him.

"No wonder Ernest wasn't available," she said, pulling off the bathing cap, auburn hair spilling out, "when I needed a ride home."

"Señora Silva gave you a lift, then?"

She nodded.

He asked, perhaps too lightly, "What did you two girls talk about?"

"Not much. The general rode with us."

"My abrupt departure must have come up."

"It did. I explained that since your retirement from British Intelligence, you at times have difficulties in crowds. You get anxious."

He smiled. "Well-played. Did they buy it?"

An owl screeched as if expressing a skeptical opinion.

"I wasn't sure at first," she said. "But when they realized Ernest wasn't waiting out front, and that you'd likely had him take you back here, any doubts they might have seemed moot."

"But I *wasn't* here when they brought you back."

"No, but some lights were on. They assumed you were here, I guess, and at any rate didn't bother confirming it."

A breeze ruffled leaves; he would not allow himself any paranoia, although the Walther was wrapped in a nearby towel.

"Or perhaps," Sand said, "they knew of Leonardo's presence, and thought he'd removed...the problem. That is, me."

Her head tilted to one side. "You think that's possible?"

"Don't you?" He took her hand. He pulled her to him. "You *are* a nimble female, Mrs. Sand."

"Is that a comment on my bedroom abilities?"

"More your out-of-the-bedroom abilities. I would say you'd make a pretty fair spy yourself."

Her half-smile had a wickedness about it. "Is that what you were doing at the Pearl, with all that shameless flirting with the First Lady? Spying?"

He shrugged the question off. "That was mostly her."

"You sound like a child—'*she* started it!'"

"Well, she did." He squeezed her hand. "Any flirting in return I might have done was strictly in the line of duty."

"*Might* have done?"

"Did," he admitted.

"You're wise not to fudge. I know what happened. I was there. I saw."

And his wife didn't even know about what had occurred under the table!

She was frowning at him now, but no irritation was in it at all. "Did you notice how General Barrios reacted to that foolishness?"

"My attention was on Señora Silva—out of politeness, of course."

"Yes, and that plunging neckline. You *really* didn't notice?"

Sand shrugged. "He did seem rather dour as dinner wore on."

"Not dour, John—*jealous.*"

He huffed a laugh. "Jealous? Not just a *soldier*, loyal to her husband, the *Presidente*? Offended by the First Lady so openly flirting?"

She considered that for a moment, then shook her head,

the auburn locks damp at their tips, touching her shoulders. "No, I could see the signs, John."

"Of what?"

"An affair."

His nod came slow, but he did nod. She was right. He should have seen it. Of course, what man wouldn't be distracted, with the voluptuous First Lady rubbing his tux pants where they buttoned in front?

He said, "An affair could well be a non-political motive for getting her husband out of the way."

"Maybe not *entirely* non-political—Isabella would be in power, and at her side would be the top military man in San Ignacio."

"But," Sand said, "if they were to rid themselves of Silva, and got found out, rival factions in their country could cry coup...and then stage their own."

"So they hired it done," she said, agreeing. "Using a freelance assassin with ties to the CIA, and therefore the USA."

"And sweep into power," he said, eyes tight with thought, "unquestioned."

"Do we care?"

He blinked. "You mean, they might be doing this not just out of passion, but to take advantage and close a hugely profitable deal with Boldt Oil?"

She nodded. Somewhere in the night, a bird trilled its at once solemn and sweet song.

"You are a ruthless child," he said with a respectful grin. "And a brilliant one."

"So what will you do?"

"What would you have me do?"

"You came as Kennedy's emissary and, frankly, his private secret agent. Double-crossing the President of the

United States is probably not a good idea."

"Probably not," he granted. "Bad for business."

"And, frankly, I wouldn't trust that female Machiavelli farther than I could throw her, which wouldn't be far, since she probably weighs one-hundred-and-fifty pounds. That's about eleven stone to you."

"A bit catty of you to say so, but probably accurate. That bosom certainly weighs heavily on me."

She elbowed him, but she was smiling.

"So what do we do now?" she asked him.

"Well, I should probably try to learn if President Silva is still alive, and if so, determine what is needed to keep him that way."

"How would you do that?"

"Just drop by the palace unannounced. And unseen."

A nighthawk on the wing gave a nasal cry.

She squeezed his hand. "We'll go together."

"No. With the security I'll be up against, it'll be tricky enough for one. Two would be a crowd, I'm afraid."

Her eyebrows were up. "I'm just to stay here and worry?"

"Stay here and think."

"About?"

"About what you would tell our jealous general and randy First Lady, should I get caught. Perhaps you could convince them that my retirement anxiety issues include occasional sleepwalking."

"Maybe you should just *not* get caught."

"I'll bear that in mind."

They went back into the cottage and Sand changed into an all-black ensemble—rubber-soled shoes, slacks, and a thin turtleneck, his Walther transferred from towel to shoulder-holster. He tucked Glace's switchblade in his sock and a backup .22 in an ankle holster.

She walked him out the door with a whispered, "Take care, Mr. Sand."

"Always, Mrs. Sand."

Then he kissed her, brief enough not to worry her, lingering enough for her to take seriously.

She slipped inside as he made his way into the dense tropical foliage making up the gardens of Silva's compound. Armed guards patrolled the drives, the perimeter of the building, and the wall; but otherwise the gardens seemed to belong to Sand and a few assorted smaller creatures. No real threat among the latter, though he knew of a few poisonous species of snake endemic to San Ignacio. He watched where he stepped. Running into a Fer-de-Lance would have been unfortunate.

No opportunity had presented itself, earlier, for Sand to determine the routes of the guards and the timing of their circuits—armed men might show up anytime, anywhere. His only friend was the darkness—the surrounding grounds were not lighted at all—which meant he had to be back at the cottage before daylight.

After five minutes of creeping under low-hanging leaves, pausing behind trees, and freezing whenever a sentry wandered near his path, Sand was dirty, sweaty, and still a good twenty yards short of the palace. Though the front of the structure was lit up like Buckingham Palace at night, the rear was limited to roving searchlights at left and right whose positioning left plenty of shadows for Sand to slip into, as long as he could cross twenty yards of open grass without automatic weapons mowing him down.

Still enjoying the seclusion of tropical undergrowth, Sand could take time to study the crisscross pattern of the searchlights. As with an automobile's blind spot, a narrow swath in the darkness blocked him from view for a span of one...two...three...four...five seconds. Would that give him time to rise, cut across the distance, and disappear into the safe shadows?

It was what he had to work with, and would have to do.

His next problem was a guard dogging his duty, taking a cigarette break on the path to Sand's right. The window of opportunity came and went three times with the guard smoking and staring absently right at the stretch of grass that Sand needed to fill unseen. Every moment wasted here waiting was a moment closer to capture. Finally, his fingers searched out a small rock, no bigger than a golf ball; maybe it was enough to buy him the time he needed....

Five seconds before the five seconds he needed, Sand turned onto his side, so silently it impressed even him, held his breath, picked a flight path, and threw the rock, sending it between two branches, neither of which the projectile touched at all. It arced over the guard and into the tropical plants beyond, landing with a satisfying rustle of leaves. The guard swung in that direction, tossed his cigarette, brought his rifle up, and took off that way, hunched somewhat, as if moving into battle.

Sand launched himself at a full sprint, traversing the open ground, waiting for a cry of alarm to be raised or a round to knock him off his feet and onto the manicured lawn to feel the warm, spreading numbness of a bullet wound. Instead, he disappeared into the shadows at the base of the wall of the palace.

He breathed again. For a few seconds, in fact, he just crouched in blessed shadow, regulating his breathing.

With his back to the cold limestone, he edged toward the center of the building, where two sentries were posted at a wide veranda. He intended to free-climb the dark wall before he got that far. Sneaking in through a door or first floor window was not viable option—doing so would surely get him caught.

But Presidente Silva, or at least his architect, hadn't considered limestone's lack of smoothness, which made scaling a building a snap to a skilled climber like John Sand. The security here was set up to keep intruders away, with little if any plan, apparently, should someone get as far as he had now.

He reached up, found purchase with his gloveless fingers, pulled himself up, got a foothold, stopped and listened. A faint rustle of breeze in leaves and nothing more. His right hand snaked up, found a spot, his left did the same, gripping, then the opposite foot rose and found a point that held. Again, he remained still and listened. Silence. He repeated the process. Again. Slow going, but there was no rush—these shadows, missed by the searchlights, weren't going anywhere.

But he was.

Sweat ran down his face and his perspiration-soaked turtleneck clung to him; his fingers burned, his toes ached, but he kept climbing, climbing, climbing all the way to the third floor where a tall dark double window waited. Once he was even with the aperture, he peeked through uncurtained glass to the darkened room, which seemed to be vacant, though he could not be sure.

His feet positioned well, hanging by one hand, he used Glace's switchblade on the seam of the tall French door-style windows and snapped the cheap window lock, pushing the pane so that it swung into the room. He slipped through and in, glad for a floor under him, and dropped to his hands and knees, every muscle aching. Soon he rose and closed the window, relieved he still had the strength to do that simple chore before any of the guards out back had happened to glance up and see it open.

He appeared to have selected a guest bedroom. His night vision and moonlight got together to reveal a four-poster king-sized bed with white duvet and pillows, and a cherry wood table, dresser, and armoire. But the room felt unused to him.

Scaling the wall had tested his strength—over a year away from active duty had taken its toll—but getting here would be a holiday compared to the descent, unless of course he just fell, in which case the return trip wouldn't be hard at all, just the landing. Well, that was a worry for another time, perhaps half an hour from now.

The current objective was to find Presidente Silva, sooner not later. Entry on the second floor would have taxed him less, but the third floor made the most sense as the level where Silva was likely hidden away. The first floor was for hosting parties, and the day-to-day meetings, as well as the kitchen and formal dining room. The second floor would be offices and meeting rooms. It stood to reason this floor would be the residence. The guidebook he'd studied on the plane to San Ignacio said the palace's three floors had four corridors built around an atrium. Eight rooms in each corridor, four to a side. Thirty-two rooms... and Silva could be in any one.

Switchblade in hand, he went to the door and listened, heard nothing, then cracked it open. The corridor lights had been dimmed, not surprising at this time of night. He eased into the hallway, moving along with his back to the wall. He doubted he'd encounter guards. If Isabella were regularly playing rumpy-pumpy with General Barrios, they'd hardly want an audience around.

He moved along with his back to the wall, skirting the

occasional chair or other small item of furniture, checking rooms, finding only darkness and silence. After half a dozen empty chambers, his nerves were getting frayed and he was beginning to doubt his approach to the problem.

He had come full circle, or rather square, and was only a few doors away from the room he'd entered through. He had his hand on the first door on this corridor and was about to twist it when, beyond the door, a female voice moaned, "*Aí, Papi! Papi!*"

"*Mamá!*" came a male voice. "*Mamá!*"

He released the knob as if a snake from that tropical garden were in his grasp. This was not Eden, however, although the general who'd spoken to him of the devil's playground was surely within that room with the First Lady.

Sand moved on to the next door, but then voices and footsteps echoed in the atrium from the adjoining corridor at left. With someone coming, he couldn't take time to check if the room was empty or occupied, and had to take his chances and slip within. As the voices of approaching guards grew louder, and louder, until they were directly outside his door, he traded the switchblade for the Walther.

Then the guards and their conversation began to recede, soon fading to almost nothing, and that was when he heard something else: light snoring.

Enough moonlight was leaking through the curtains to reveal a man in a hospital gown, asleep.

President Jose Silva.

El Presidente slept fitfully in a hospital bed near the window and the moonlight, an IV bottle on a stand hovering, its needle attached to the back of his hand, which lay over a sheet gathered at his waist.

The manner in which President Silva was receiving care was not befitting the leader of his country, or any country—his long, unkempt black hair spread out like nasty seaweed on his soiled pillow; his salt-and-pepper mustache untrimmed and drooping; his wrinkled, sweat-reeking hospital gown hiding much of the sickly gray pallor of his flesh.

The president's eyes opened slowly, as if the effort to do so took every last bit of his strength.

In a harsh dry whisper, Silva said, "*Eres tu, puta?*"

Well, Sand thought, *if 'Is that you, whore?' is how he greets the First Lady, then the romance is definitely out of the Silva marriage.*

As Sand approached, the patient's eyes widened upon seeing a stranger in his room, and somehow he managed to sit up. Sand clapped a hand over Silva's mouth, the president's eyes bulging as he feebly struggled to pry the fingers loose, with bony hands, one of which had that IV needle taped to it. But the contents of the IV were apparently not medicine, rather something designed to dull the strength from the not yet fifty-year-old body.

Leaning close, Sand whispered, "Mr. President, it's John Sand—do you remember me?"

Silva continued to struggle, not that Sand expended any great effort restraining this husk of a human.

"We met once, years ago," Sand continued, sotto voce, hand still over the man's mouth, "when I was with MI6. We *have* met, you *know* me. I mean you no harm."

Silva goggled at this night visitor, his struggles ebbing as fast as what remained of his energy. Then a glimmer of recognition came to the dark eyes. The feeble battling ceased and, finally, the orbs above Sand's hand softened, seemed even to focus...

...and Silva managed a tiny nod.

Sand asked, "May I safely remove my hand?"

A slightly stronger nod.

But Sand left his hand at Silva's chin level, ready to resume his grip.

Silva whispered hoarsely, "I...I remember you."

"Who's doing this to you, Mr. President?"

"Water...please...."

From the nightstand, Sand brought a glass with an angled straw to Silva's lips. The patient sipped. A swallow, another sip, another swallow. Then a nod for Sand to take the glass away.

"My wife, the whore," Silva said, and a touch of what must have been his old strength rose in his voice, "and General Barrios, the traitor. They are responsible. They intend to take control of San Ignacio. With me helpless, and bedridden...what can I do to stop them?"

"In your present condition, nothing. But perhaps I can."

"What is MI6's interest in this?"

"I no longer work for them. I represent several parties. First, my wife is Stacey Boldt, CEO of Boldt oil."

Something came alive in his eyes.

"I'm also on a mission of sorts," Sand said, "for Fidel Castro."

And died in those eyes.

"Then you are here to...*kill* me, Mr. Sand?"

"No. The opposite, sir. Castro told me he tried to warn you, but that you didn't listen."

"...This is true."

"But I also represent President Kennedy."

The eyes came alive again.

"Castro and Kennedy—strange bedfellows," said the man to this strange fellow at his bedside.

"They both want to keep the Russians out of the Caribbean," Sand said. "But there's no time now for geopolitics.

You're scheduled to make a major address soon, yes?"

Life was flowing through Silva again, despite what might be in the IV.

El Presidente said, "I will propose the Caribbean Island Trade Union...an organization allowing all member islands to trade freely with each other, and to profit from everyone else's trade policies. Those doing well could assist others who may not be as fortunate."

"A high tide raising all boats," Sand said.

"That is my hope. And the plan that I intend to share with my neighbor countries, if I am able to speak. But Isabella and Barrios, they are greedy....They want our island's wealth for themselves."

Sand said, "If you're allowed to give that speech, that's likely when you'll be assassinated."

And Isabella, blood-spattered and shattered at his side, would never be suspected...even when she and her lover took over the country.

"What can be done, Mr. Sand?"

"I'm going to stop the bitch, Mr. President," Sand said. "And her bastard."

"God bless you!" Silva tried to gather himself and it was, for all his renewed life, pitiful. "Now get me out of here...and we'll retake my country!"

How far this drugged man had managed to rally himself was an incredible thing to witness. But Sand cautioned him with a gently raised palm.

"We can't do that, sir. If I try to remove you from here, in your condition, we would almost certainly both be killed."

"What do you propose?"

"You're going to have to put up with these indignities for another day or two. Is there anything *really* wrong with you?"

"No! They're sedating me. I know they are."

"Then remove the IV needle. Just leave it unattached under the bandage. If they notice, they will reapply it, thinking it came loose. Then remove it again and keep that up as long as you can."

"All right. All right."

Sand touched and gripped a thin arm. "Sir, I promise you, we'll stop them."

Silva, resolved, nodded. "I understand. I'm depending on you, Mr. Sand."

"I will do my best, Mr. President."

Sand's watch told him barely an hour remained before dawn. Getting back to the cottage was going to be even more difficult than he'd thought. But it had to be done.

So much had to be done.

CHAPTER FOURTEEN
WITHOUT A STACE

Dawn was hugging the eastern horizon like distant wildfire as Sand slipped into the cottage, going in back by the pool, relieved not to be seen by a uniformed solider on patrol checking the little cluster of cottages on the blacktop apron. The return from the palace had been smoother than he'd anticipated, but pausing for safety at various stops along the way had dragged things out.

A tousled Stacey, still in the Givenchy gown and atop their bed where she'd finally caught some sleep, said, "What on—"

He held a finger to his lips, by way of reminder, indicating the bugged bedside lamp.

She nodded, blinking herself further awake, her expression tight with query and concern.

In a fake yawn, he said, "Good morning, dear—sleep well?"

Mildly disgusted at having to play this game, Stacey said, "Like a rock, sweetheart...and you?"

"Ah, I woke up with that kink in my shoulder again."

"You think maybe a hot shower would help?"

"Just might," he allowed, stripping out of his dirty, sweat-dampened clothes, and Stacey got out of the now very rumpled gown.

In the warm but not steaming shower, he filled her in, though truncating his various perilous difficulties while not stinting on the conversation with Silva.

"You make it sound so easy," she said over the drumming shower, "for a man whose fifteen-minute conversation took four hours."

"We can waste time discussing what a heroic so-and-so I am, *or* I can outline my thoughts on saving President Silva."

"Yes, maybe that instead."

When he'd finished, she shook her head skeptically, scattering droplets.

"Problem?" he asked.

"Barrios won't be sorry you're among the missing, John, but the First Lady will have a cow."

"You'll just have to midwife her then. Try the speech about their need to deal with the president of the company and not the 'hired help.'"

"Isabella may bridle."

"She's scheduled an all-day meeting, correct?"

"Correct."

"Tell her I'll miss only the morning session. That you've dispatched me to touch bases with the American consulate. Which enjoys the benefit of being more or less true."

"It does," she admitted. Her apprehension was again exaggerated by water running down her face like tears.

He said, "We'll meet back here for lunch."

They embraced. That it didn't lead anywhere emphasized the seriousness of the situation.

Dried and dressed, they went their separate ways—Stacey, in a black flare-trousered jumpsuit by Yves Saint Laurent, was ferried by golf cart to the palace, while Sand was met at their door by Ernest with the limo.

Sand, in a white linen suit, climbed in back for the ride to the American consulate. He and Ernest exchanged pleasantries about the nice breeze mitigating the heat, and along the way the chauffeur pointed out a few of San Ignacio's sights. Sand treated himself to a *Gauloises*.

Twenty minutes later, he was in the lobby of the consulate—just off the downtown with its touristy bustle, not far from where he and Leonardo had run a foot race not starting with a firing gun but ending with one.

He presented his ID to the Marine guard and soon was in the private office of the consul, a gaunt gent named MacDonald who had managed, despite working on a Caribbean island, a pasty-faced complexion that his dark gray suit emphasized. Since he'd been expected, Sand was quickly set up with a private telephone in an unused office.

He dialed the memorized number and waited.

Moments later, a familiar presidential voice responded: "This is Lancer."

The Secret Service code name for JFK.

Sand got right to it, explaining the Silva situation and asking for help.

A long pause followed, filled only with faint long-distance crackle, before Kennedy said, "John, I need to leave this in your, uh, experienced hands."

Sand had frankly expected this. The Bay of Pigs fiasco had been barely two months before, so dispatching American forces to San Ignacio, even at Silva's request, was something the President could hardly risk. And Sand wouldn't have made this island trip, if Kennedy trusted the CIA.

"In which case," Sand said matter of fact, "you can disavow me."

The President didn't equivocate. "Yes, John. I'm sorry, but you know the position I'm in. You do this for your adopted country, and I will, uh, make sure it's not forgotten."

Ask not what your adopted country can do for you, ask what you can do....

The secret agent said, "I will do my best, Mr. President."

Riding back to the palace compound, engaging in no small talk with Ernest on the return trip, Sand brooded over just how exactly he and his oil company bride might, on their own devices, stop a presidential assassination. He'd been in similar situations while at MI6, the Home Office having no problem leaving him with the proverbial sticky wicket. But this time was different—this time his wife's safety, her *life*, was at risk, no matter how little he managed not to involve her directly.

And yet with her brains, her Cuchillo-trained skills, and a captain of industry's nerves, she represented the only help, the only back-up, he could call upon. His male urge to protect her fought with his cold professional awareness that she was just the right "man" for the job.

And a way forward was formulating, bubbling like something on a stove waiting for just the last few right ingredients....

By the time Ernest dropped him off at the cottage, Sand didn't have all the details down, but had more than the glimmer of a plan. A picnic-style lunch of sandwiches and crisps, sent over from the palace, was waiting with Stacey when he entered.

"Let's take this outside," he suggested, "and enjoy the lovely day."

They sat at a small round metal table by the pool, a table

inspected for, and found free of, electronic bugs of course. They nibbled at their crab-salad sandwiches as he brought her up to speed on Kennedy's disappointing response.

"You had to try," she said.

"I did, but I understand his position. He's vulnerable after the Cuban muck-up. We're on our own, but we'll do what we need to do."

"I'm included in your plans?" she said, pleasantly surprised. "Not just assigned to sit by the window with a lighted lamp?"

"More like a Molotov cocktail. Care to report on the meeting with Señora Silva?"

Stacey's laugh was deep and harsh, like a man's. "The First Lady came ready to make you dance to her tune, as she does with all men—in no way prepared for a negotiation with another woman...even less so after I took your advice and made the speech about Boldt Oil being mine and all decisions likewise. Her terms were ridiculous and I told her so."

"And what were those terms, my love?"

"She made your late friend Trujillo seem the soul of reason."

"*Ay caramba*, as the natives say."

Stacey, looking past him, raised a palm for him to halt their conversation. He turned and saw a green-uniformed soldier approaching, having come around the side of the cottage.

Sand asked, "*Te puedo ayudar?*"

Can I help you?

The soldier stopped. "Señora Silva is asking for you, Señor Sand. There is news *importante* about *el Presidente*. Would you come, sir?"

"Of course," Sand said, rising, as did Stacey.

But the soldier said, "My apologies, Señora. My orders are to collect only Señor Sand."

"Of course," Stacey said warmly, her eyes cold.

Sand kissed his wife's cheek, whispered, "Won't be long."

"Wham, bam, thank you, Sand?"

He let her have the last word, following the soldier to a waiting golf cart. Shortly Sand was following his escort up the limestone steps and into the palace. The soldier led him through the expansive marble entryway and around to an elevator to escort him to the third floor, down the very corridor and to the room where not so long ago he had nearly interrupted Isabella and her favorite general.

The soldier knocked on the heavy wooden door, though it had not been heavy enough on Sand's last visit to entirely muffle the carnal goings-on behind it.

Isabella's voice came, rather bored: "*Entré.*"

In moments—sealed within the First Lady's private quarters—Sand was taking in the plush surroundings of a chamber twice the size of the captive President Silva's makeshift hospital room.

On the facing wall, at left, loomed a life-sized, gilt-framed oil portrait of Isabella, quite well done, with a tiny San Ignacio at her feet—it was as if *King Kong* had starred Fay Wray and Manhattan had been Queenstown. This fantasy First Lady wore a red off-the-shoulder gown, her ebony hair piled high, neck bedecked with a diamond necklace of unfathomable karats. The mammoth portrait hovered over the foot of a golden Rococo double bed with royal blue silk comforter and pillowcases. Apparently what Isabella wanted to see, first thing every morning, was herself at her beautiful best, towering over her citizens.

Something to shoot for.

Right now, however, in the flesh as they say, the First Lady reclined on a maroon chaise draped along a pair of tall French-style windows, opposite him as he moved deeper into the room. Her pink silk robe had been flipped open with studious casualness to display long, rather muscular (but not masculine) legs. She raised herself on an elbow, appraising the guest she'd summoned. A glimpse of black fringe where her thighs met and the twin hard tips of her full bosom conspired to let him know nothing lay between the pink of the robe and the coffee-with-cream hills and valleys underneath.

Somehow he doubted this had been Señora Silva's wardrobe this morning, when she met with Stacey (formerly Boldt) Sand. But he would definitely not inquire of his wife if that had been the case.

Unlike in her portrait, her black tresses were down, falling to her shoulders, obsidian waterfalls framing her strong, lovely features. Her smile was a scarlet gash in her oval face, a spectacular wound.

"Ah, Señor Sand. What a pleasure it is to see you again."

"Delightful to see you again, Señora Silva," he said, taking a tentative step toward her.

"I had thought we established you would call me Isabella."

"Then please call me 'John,' Isabella."

She swung herself slowly into a seated position, and along the way the dark tufted triangle the fringe had hinted at was, in a brief flash, confirmed.

"When you were absent from our meeting this morning," she said, "I was afraid I had somehow...*offended* you last night. That I had perhaps been too forward...but I have always been a woman who hides little about what she feels. Perhaps this may be seen as a weakness for a member of the ruling class."

"Not at all. It just means you have things in common with the, uh, commoners."

She patted the chaise next to her. "Join me, would you?"

"Certainly."

As he settled next to her, leaving some space between them, she giggled. It didn't suit her. She was not the giggling type and it only revealed the contrivance, like a magician with a dove peeking out of a pocket.

"You seem uncomfortable," she said. "These is no need. You say those novels about you are somewhat embellished—does that include bedroom exploits?"

He kept his smile modest in several senses. "Isabella, please do not confuse me with a fictional character. I assure you my physiological reaction to you is quite real."

"I can see as much," she said, her eyes not on his face.

"But I am a married man," he said. "Contentedly so. And I have no wish to compromise that union, or any bond between your country and my wife's oil company."

"I understand, John. I really do. But we are strong people, all of us. You. Your wife. Myself."

"Your husband."

"Yes. My husband. But if we are to forge an alliance, John, you and I...we need a bond. A strong, behind-the-scenes bond, the kind of which only a man and a woman are capable." She shrugged. "I am perhaps an old-fashioned girl when it comes to business."

There was little about Isabella Silva that was old-fashioned, except perhaps in an age-old way going back to Eve and her descendants Cleopatra and Mata Hari.

"As for my husband..." she said, and contempt came into her tone. "I will show the depth of my seriousness, John. I will share with you my terrible secret. My husband...he is weak."

"Ill, you mean."

The dark eyes flared. "Of spirit! Spineless and coward-ly. He would give all our country's riches away. He would gladly be your president's lapdog! San Ignacio deserves more, deserves better! *I* deserve *so* much more...."

He smiled, allowing a hint of mockery in. "Is that why you took General Barrios to your bed?"

For a moment, her expression was as if she'd had a glass of cold water splashed in her lovely face. But that passed and she displayed a peculiar combination of cool and warm, saying, "I should have expected as much from a man with your background, of your experience...you are as observant as the finest detective, John."

He flipped a hand. "Barrios would seem to be a strong man. Capable of stepping in, if your husband is the weak-ling you say. Military coups happen all of the time in your part of the world."

"They do," she admitted, "and the general *is* strong. Perhaps too strong. I suspect he uses me for his own ends."

"How so?"

"It is as you say—I foresee a military coup. I would outlive my usefulness and he would have me, as they say, 'disappeared.'"

He didn't buy that for a minute, but was her judgment wrong about Barrios, or was this was part of pulling Sand's strings—who could say? Yet he felt Stacey was right about Barrios. For the general, the affair was as much about lust-ful love as greedy power grab.

"Isn't his strength a good thing?" Sand asked, trying to ignore the hand that now stroked his thigh.

"I need a strong man who can lead *with* me. *You* could be that man."

She let the robe drop from her shoulders to gather at her waist, exposing the smooth copper-hued curves. Her breasts had a cantaloupe roundness with small, almost sharp points in areolas that had been rouged with the same make-up applied to those bruised, blood-red lips.

Almost purring, she said, "The position *would* have its benefits, after all."

Isabella leaned in and kissed him on the mouth, sliding her arms around him, pressing against him. He let it play out, even when her tongue snaked in his mouth to have a look around.

There had been a time, a day—or more accurately, nights—when John Sand would gladly, gratefully accept the charms of women whose beauty housed evil, treachery or other flaws one in his line of work often encountered. Passing fancies, one might say. Dangerous but better than ducking bullets.

With his hands firmly on her arms, he moved her away. Rose. "That was very nice. You do that well, Isabella. But you must have missed it when I mentioned my wife. And the way to her oil rights is not through her husband's trousers."

To her credit, he thought, she did not take offense. No hissing or throwing things. She'd made her play and, for once, the house hadn't won.

"She is a lucky woman," Isabella said. "May I make a suggestion?"

He was at the door. "Certainly."

"Do not share with her the nature of our negotiations, you and I. And do not take everything I say seriously. You are not a man easily fooled—I suspect those books about you are not as exaggerated as you say. But believe me when I tell you that I am in love with my husband, however weak he may be. I am just a woman with needs, with hungers, who likes the occasional general or former secret agent in her life. It keeps things interesting...and Isabella young."

"I believe you," he said with a smile, thinking, *as far as I could throw you, you eleven-stone Dragon Lady.*

A golf cart conveyed him back to the cottage. Along the way he was wrestling with how much if anything he should share with Stacey about the First Lady's shameless seduction attempt. He would certainly at least leave out that he'd had a raging erection through much of it—that might seem to undercut a husband's steadfast loyalty to a wife.

When he entered the cottage, Stacey wasn't there, but someone else was—a nondescript blond fellow, a face in the crowd, who—judging by the fresh look of his charcoal suit—either was staying at a hotel with quick dry-cleaning service, or had multiples of the same unimpressive, off-the-rack suit.

Genuinely impressive, however, was the silenced .45 automatic, an overwhelming weapon for an average hand, trained on Sand, who slowly moved into the small living room, to face the assassin seated in a rattan chair.

Pleasant, smiling a little, Lenny Warner said, "Have a seat, John."

"You should have already shot me," Sand said. "Talking with a target is an amateur move."

"You're not my target, John. We were friends once, remember?"

"No. We did two jobs. That was enough."

"Sit, would you?"

Sand pulled up another rattan chair. Close enough to jump this bastard, if the chance came. "If you think you have me—"

"But I don't *need* you, John." Leonardo's smile turned up the sadistic wattage. "Not when I've got your wife."

Sand's hands became fists. That big bulky noise-suppressed automatic was aimed at his head; the sound would be minimal, the usual cough; but this close up, Sand's head would explode into chunks. Closed casket, definitely.

And no help for Stacey.

He would stay calm.

"What do you want for her, Lenny?"

"We'll get to that. First, like slow motion in the movies, take your Walther out of the shoulder rig and toss it on that couch. On the cushion, nice and easy. Wouldn't want it going off."

Using two fingers, Sand obeyed.

"Nicely professional," Leonardo said. "Now, the .22 in your ankle holster. Same routine. Listen, old friend, you can live through this, really. So can Stacey."

It was pointless to ask, but he heard himself saying, "Where do you have her?"

"John, please. You know you're not in charge. Don't embarrass yourself. The little woman is safe. She is, in fact, with a mutual friend."

"What? Who?"

Leonardo's smile turned sideways; he smiled a lot for a man devoid of humor or any noticeable humanity. "Your faithful driver. Your loyal guide."

Sand swallowed. "Ernest."

"Ernest, yes! But he saved your worthless ass, you're thinking. A man of your talents, your experience, and yet such a streak of naivete! It's adorable. Those missions we worked together—you've *seen* me shoot. Do you honestly think I could miss you from that distance?"

Sand had assumed that the headlights from the car blinded the shooter, but had they...?

"I'm embarrassed to say," Leonardo said, "but the timing of our little charade was off, a tad. I actually got off two shots before Ernest hit his lights. He was a hair late. Turned out it didn't matter. Retired only a year, and you're already soft. Your edge gone. Your radar permanently on the fritz. How easy it was to put a man close to you. Someone you came quickly to trust. Someone who you soon let your guard down around."

Leonardo was not wrong.

The chatty assassin continued: "I was pretty sure, this soon after *Playa Girón,* that Kennedy wouldn't risk interfering in our plans. But when you exited the consulate today, I *knew.* I could read the disappointment on your face, and right then I realized we could go ahead unhindered."

"If so, why am I still alive, Lenny? Why terrorize Stacey?"

Other than the general sickness in your soul....

"Two reasons, John. You're something of a minor celebrity now, in some circles at least, and killing you might make for an international incident, and those kind of headlines...who needs them? Secondly, you are here doing the bidding of JFK himself, and you may have reported my part in this to him already. That might initiate efforts to track me down and liquidate my sunny self, which I definitely do not want or need. And, of course, we *are* old friends...."

"Buddies," Sand said dryly.

"Sarcasm aside, let's invoke professional courtesy. I'm giving you the opportunity to walk out of this with your life and, if you behave, your wife."

"That would be optimal."

"Wouldn't it, you British prick? As I said, Stacey is with Ernest. I think of him as my protégé, John, so don't underestimate him—he's damn near as good as I am. I hesitate to mention this, but Ernest—despite his cheerful demeanor—has a special talent for inflicting pain, when the situation calls for it."

"What do you want from me, Lenny?"

Leonardo's voice finally had outright nastiness in it. "Go home, Sand. Right the hell now. Keep your head down and your mouth shut. In one week, this will all be over, and I will send rich little Stacey home to you, absolutely no worse for wear."

"And should I refuse?"

"I'll kill you here and now—or, later, if you buy time by pretending to cooperate. Either way, Ernest kills Stacey, but slowly, painfully."

"If I were dead, why would that be necessary?"

"Well, we have to get rid of—oh. You mean, why *torture* her, if you are already gone? I guess to make your agony not just physical. For the sheer fun of it. Trust me, Ernest enjoys that aspect of things as much as I do. Know that even after your death, he will *truly* make her suffer."

"You are one sick son of a bitch, Lenny."

"I suppose I'm like a smoker whose taste buds have been dulled. Only tabasco sauce rings the bell. The suffering of others has to be *intense* for me to feel it."

"I will do as you say," Sand said. "I will fly to Houston. If Stacey's not returned, unharmed, I will track you and kill you and, believe me, it will be intense enough for you to feel it."

He laughed a little. He liked that.

"But humor me, Lenny—why Silva?"

He shrugged a shoulder—not the gun-hand one. "For

the same reason as Trujillo. Silva just didn't want to do business reasonably. Castro showed my employers that if such people are allowed to think for themselves, decades of business and investment will go down the crapper. *You* tried to deal with Trujillo. *You* know what he wanted for oil rights on that chickenshit island of his. I mean, you weren't going to pay the freight, were you?"

"No," Sand confirmed.

"You put a greedy, grasping son of a bitch like that in a room with Silva, with his desire to start a Caribbean trade union, and the next thing you have is higher prices on everything, not just oil. There's a lot of business being done on these islands, John. Casinos, sugar, rum, oil. When these lowlife wogs forget their place, suddenly prices are sky high. Tourists stop traveling to casinos. Castro screwed this up for everybody, and Trujillo, if he lived, woulda made it worse. And this bum Silva is a goddamned do-gooder, and that's a real recipe for disaster."

Sand was shaking his head. "What makes you think Isabella would be any easier to deal with? What she wanted from my wife for oil rights made a piker out of Trujillo."

"The First Lady was just yanking your honey's chain. There's nobody a good-looking broad like Isabella hates more than a *better*-looking broad...meaning no disrespect to your lady, John. But Isabella baby is pragmatic, and is up for doing business at a reasonable cost. We can all do business together—gambling, girls, junk...and oil. All the things that make the world go round. John. Please. Shall we all just be friends again?"

CHAPTER FIFTEEN
SAND DEVIL

Sand's face was a drooping, defeated thing, indicating he'd given up, desperation to save his young wife overriding any other consideration—a has-been smothered by failure, outsmarted every step of the way by a superior foe; a winner turned loser better off staying retired and out of the game.

This was what he wanted Lenny Warner, the legendary Leonardo, to see.

But Sand's mind was alive, snarling hot, cunning cold, and inwardly he was poised like a panther waiting to strike.

Lulled by the sight of an obviously vanquished opponent, Leonardo said with a smile, "Enough discussion, don't you think, John? Time has come for you to fly home and wait for your sweet wife's return. To enjoy a happy retirement, a life of luxury, enjoying what years are left to you, secure in the knowledge that you did the right thing. Who cares what happens to one tinpot dictator or another?"

"I only care about Stacey," he said, with a sad shrug.

But Sand knew that, as it stood, she was either dead already or doomed to be, just as assassins would be waiting for his return to American soil.

Leonardo got up. "On your feet, John. Nice and easy." Sand took his time.

"We'll be off to the airport now," Leonardo said. "I have a ticket for you. No need for luggage. We'll keep things simple. I have a driver waiting."

That defined the arena. Any confrontation needed to happen within the walls of this small cottage, otherwise a second adversary would be added by way of the driver.

Leonardo gestured with the bulky silenced .45. "After you, old friend."

Sand took a painfully slow step toward the door and Leonardo moved in behind him, jabbing the weapon into his captive's spine.

"No stalling, John."

The gun's snout eased off, but Sand now knew its relative position. He reached out with his right hand for the knob of the door, in near slow motion, and that gun snout jabbed him again.

Sand swung his left elbow behind him, catching Leonardo's gun arm, and the assassin reflexively fired, sending two *thunk*ing shots into the floor, the coughs of the sound-suppressed weapon unlikely to alert the driver outside. Sand whirled and smashed his right fist into the assassin's face, breaking the man's nose, the snap like a board breaking in two.

Leonardo staggered back, blood streaming from his nostrils and dripping over a mouth whose grimace of pain, disappointment and surprise was a delightful thing to see.

But Leonardo had managed not to drop the pistol, and the threat of it waited only for the second or so it would take the killer to regain himself. So Sand lurched forward, throwing his right forearm into Leonardo's neck, which loosened the man's grip into fingers, the heavy weapon bouncing to the floor, landing God knew where.

Dazed, Leonardo nonetheless sent two swift hard lefts into Sand's kidney.

Then the two men backed away from each other. In moments the adversaries in the small living room were standing a few feet apart, facing off, both breathing hard, though only one had been bloodied so far.

Leonardo managed to smile through the scarlet mask, revealing the madness behind the face-in-the-crowd. The blow to the assassin's throat only allowed a rasping excuse for a voice to emerge when he said, "So, John... no deal then?"

"I'm exercising my escape clause."

Sand had assumed a boxer's stance, his feet a little farther apart than his shoulders, crouching only slightly, fists ready to make this bastard bleed some more.

"That means I get to kill you," Leonardo managed hoarsely. "And will I enjoy *that...*"

Sand smiled. "Will you?"

They circled, slow, less slow, fast now, and a small tightening around Leonardo's eyes signaled attack, the assassin pivoting, kicking, and Sand easily dodging, then spinning, delivering an elbow to the back of the neck, sending his opponent stumbling away.

Then Leonardo charged, tackling Sand at the waist. The two fell into a wicker coffee table that crunched like a cracker. For all the intensity of this hand-to-hand combat, the noise thus far had been minimal, hardly likely to alert a driver outside, for which Sand was glad—one foe at a time, please.

But in hurling himself, Leonardo had landed on top of Sand, an advantage he pressed, punching the other in the belly repeatedly, then head-butting him, before Sand could finally thrust his attacker off to tumble into a rattan lamp table, knocking it over, though it made little racket, the shade cushioning the lamp's crash.

Sand scrambled toward his antagonist, ready to kick the hell of him while he was down; but Leonardo jack-in-the-boxed up, yanking off his suit coat and, from somewhere, producing a combat knife what with looked to be a five-inch blade, light winking off its razor edge. Sand got out of his suit coat, wrapped it around his right forearm and hand, and circled left. Leonardo tried a few tentative thrusts with the blade, then lunged. Sand blocked, simultaneously landing a left to the side of the assassin's head, but a blade slash caught him below the wrapped forearm, ripping his sleeve, leaving him a two inch cut weeping scarlet.

Rolled-up jacket slipping off his arm, Sand stumbled backward, out of the living room and into the small kitchen, and Leonardo wasted no time coming after him, blade hefted. From the counter, Sand grabbed and parried with a cast-iron skillet, blocking the man's first thrust, and second. When the assassin lunged a third time, coming in low, Sand brought the skillet down on the assassin's wrist with a clang that elicited a howl as the knife hit linoleum and spun under the breakfast table.

Leonardo threw himself again at Sand, who sidestepped and grabbed him by the back of his shirt and slammed him full-body hard into the back door. The assassin slid down and Sand opened the door and dragged him outside by the shirt onto the cement by the pool, dumping the groggy killer on his side, then climbing on top of him. He began rubbing Leonardo's face against the rough cement, as if trying to sand both surfaces smooth. It left a bloody smear, and when the killer seemed about to pass out, Sand stopped, holding onto the man's hair with one hand, clutching it.

"Where are you keeping her? Where is Stacey?"

Speaking was an effort for the fallen assassin, but he took the trouble of offering Sand a physically impossible suggestion.

Sand hesitated to smash the bastard's head into the cement, because it might kill him, which would impede finding Stacey. As he was thinking such rational thoughts in the midst of irrational brutality, Sand got himself bucked off and went splashing on his backside into the cool water of the little pool.

With the cry of a wounded beast, Leonardo leapt after him, onto him, forcing him down, where they wrestled underwater, frantically pushing through their pain and exhaustion, each trying fruitlessly to gain an advantage. In the frenzied grappling, Leonardo managed to get behind and pin Sand's arm in back, pushing him down by a shoulder. As the assassin broke the surface for precious lungsful of air, Sand thrashed below, his right arm free, but the surface a few inches and a thousand miles away.

Sand went limp, as if Leonardo had won, but the killer didn't take the bait—if anything, his grip tightened. But Sand stayed slack, playing possum, dangling hand fumbling with a pant leg, fingers acquiring the switchblade at the side of a sock, snicking open the blade under water. Leonardo, busy doing his best to drown Sand, didn't perceive the fakery and paid for it when Sand swung the blade around and drove it deep between the assassin's ribs.

Leonardo let go at once, and Sand withdrew the blade and surfaced, gasping for air, then backed away from the killer. He leaned against the lip of the pool at the end near the kitchen, breathing hard. Blood from his wounded left arm was making slender shimmery filaments. But nothing to compare to Leonardo, mid-pool, standing there shakily, ribbons of scarlet leaving his body, eager to take life with them.

Sand walked through water to the killer, looked into his stunned features and said, "Where's Stacey? Tell me and I'll get help for you."

Warner said nothing and Sand shoved his head under water and held him there as more blood tendrils floated outward from their source, the rays of a dying sun.

Sand jerked the killer out of the water, and again asked, "Where *is* she?"

Leonardo had not a word to say on that subject, or any subject, his eyes open but empty. Unlike many dead artists, the worth of Leonardo's work would not rise in value. But what died with him was of enormous value to the tortured husband.

Sand let go of the assassin, a corpse now, sinking like his stone of a heart. By the time Sand had dragged himself out of the pool, the dead man was face down, floating. Lenny Warner, who had so enjoyed the suffering of others, had died too slowly for Sand's taste. But he would have to settle.

In the kitchen, he used a dish towel to dry his face and confiscated the fallen combat knife. All the while he was listening to see if any guests dropped by the cottage— roaming guards and/or that driver out front. But rattan breakage and splashing in the pool had apparently not aroused attention or suspicions.

In the bathroom, he took stock of his injuries—nothing serious enough to hamper him in his efforts to find and rescue his wife, though he quickly bandaged his arm. Then he freshened up just a little, mostly using a washcloth to remove blood, his own and Leonardo's.

Very quickly he got out of the white sodden suit and

into a dark dry one, but not a white shirt and tie, rather a black Ban-Lon. He used a bath towel to dry off the shoulder rig and ankle holster as best as he could; he wasn't sure what he might face, so he gathered the two spare 9mm magazines and the one extra .22 clip. In the upended living room, he filled the holsters with the Walther P38 and the Beretta 950 respectively. He collected Warner's .45. Two shots fired, one in the chamber, five in the clip. The weapon went in his belt, in front, buttoned under the suit coat.

As an afterthought, he took the empty briefcase from the bedroom into the kitchen, where he returned the packets of money from the freezer into their previous home. One never knew when a million in cold cash might come in handy.

Sand had no idea how many soldiers stood between him and the things he had to do, and cared only about what might hamper him now; first order of business was a visit to the First Lady of San Ignacio.

Well, not the very first.

Sand cracked the front door and peeked out. Standing beside another big black Lincoln was a uniformed soldier with a holstered sidearm; no young recruit, he was maybe thirty-five and had a troubled look—this was taking longer than expected, after all—and perhaps had been chosen in case Leonardo needed help with a dangerous charge.

Sand, briefcase in his left hand, exited the cottage, casually unbuttoning his suit coat. For a moment he thought the driver might salute, but then the solider straightened, although not in an "atten-*shun*" fashion.

The soldier took a few wary steps toward him, as Sand approached with a smile, saying, "*Tu jefe está indispuesto. El viaje al aeropuerto se pospone. Llevame al palacio.*"

Stopping perhaps four feet away, the soldier frowned

and his hand dropped to his holster, the flap of which required unsnapping to release its weapon. Sand yanked the big silenced .45 from his belt and shot him in the head.

"If that's how you want it," Sand grumbled, and stepped over him, avoiding the gory spillage from what had been the driver's head. The man had made more noise falling than the noise-suppressed handgun had making that happen. Leaning in for a look, Sand was pleased to see the keys in the ignition.

Something had gone right today, at least.

After glancing around and seeing no witnesses, Sand dragged the body into the cottage and left it in the trashed living room.

He drove to the palace, using the lane from the blacktop apron shared by the array of cottages, a ride taking perhaps three minutes within the compound walls. He left the Lincoln in the palace parking area and made the trip up the stone steps with the briefcase in hand. A pair of soldiers, much younger and less threatening than the one he'd just dispatched—though they wore sidearms as well—were on either side of the tall double doors of the entry.

"John Sand," he said, displaying his passport as the guard checked a clipboard. "I have a meeting with General Barrios and the First Lady."

The soldier checked for Sand's name, found it on the schedule, and nodded him in.

Again, soldiers and office workers were bustling on their way here and there. He crossed the atrium through filtered sunlight to an elevator and went up to the third floor; the trip was far easier and much quicker than the night before. He hoped his exit today would be just as uneventful.

He unbuttoned his suit coat, adjusted the .45 in his

waistband for easier access, then knocked at the First Lady's door.

In a business-like voice, seduction-free, Isabella Silva called, "*Entra, general.*"

The lovely Señora Silva was not lolling on her chaise, nor was she lazing on the Rococo double bed over which that astonishing portrait loomed. Rather she was perched on a cushioned stool at an art deco vanity table, still draped in the pink silk robe, touching up her make-up at its large shell-shaped mirror, in which she saw him enter.

"John!"

Imagine that—she was surprised to see him. Why, did she think something might have happened to him?

She swiveled on the stool and turned, then rose like Botticelli's Venus. From her smile you might have thought a kitten was licking her feet. "Have you had second thoughts?"

"Oh yes," he said.

She stepped away from the vanity—though she brought plenty of vanity along—and moved slowly toward him, the clinging silk emphasizing all the hills and valleys of San Ignacio. She eyed the briefcase in his left hand.

"And what do you have there, John?"

"Well, we *do* have a business meeting scheduled. Perhaps it's my notes."

That face, as strong and confident as it was beautiful, betrayed to him an edge of unease for the first time.

She said, as if cooing words of love, "I had understood that meeting was...postponed."

So. She had offered him a seat next to her throne this morning, and then sent him into Leonardo's hands, to die. She had...as he'd suspected...been party to, or at the very least facilitated, Stacey's capture.

They were close enough now to embrace, but they did not. Nor did they kiss, standing there halfway between the door and the chaise, and very near the bed where she had conducted so much business before.

"It *is* notes," he said. "Let me show you."

He advanced to the bed—the covers were turned down, though it was early afternoon; but of course a woman in her line of work had to be ready for a transaction at any time of day. He rested the briefcase on the edge of the mattress atop the blue satin comforter. He snapped the case open.

The packets of money, frosted over, were still encased in newspaper. He partially unwrapped one and a thickness of greenbacks looked out. She touched them, withdrawing her hand as if the brick of money were a burner on a hot stove, and not...

"Cold," she said, frowning.

"Cold cash," he replied pleasantly. "A million dollars. It's all yours, Isabella."

Those big dark eyes grew bigger. "Mine? Mine..."

"Just tell me where she's being kept. My wife." He gripped her arm. Hard enough to draw her attention away from a million dollars. "Where does he have her? Where can I find the charming Ernest?"

She was shaking her head, all that ebony hair bouncing off shoulders in pink silk. "I....I know nothing of this."

"You *do* know. And the money is yours if you tell me where to find her."

Dark eyes flared. "This money will be mine, John?"

"It's a down payment," he said. "We're talking business, Isabella, just as we said we would. For oil rights test drilling. There will be another million, when Mrs. Sand and I are safely away from your...delightful little island."

She looked at the money, then at him. The big dark

eyes, glittering moist, liked what they saw.

But the man who burst in, a revolver at the ready, did *not* like what he saw.

Slamming the door behind him, General Jose Barrios, in his fine uniform—confronted by the sight of John Sand standing there with Isabella Silva, the two close enough to embrace, to kiss, the general's beautiful married mistress in nothing but that clingy robe, standing next to a bed that he surely knew well—made a noise somewhere between an infant's cry and a dying man's moan, and he raised his pistol, pointing it at this bedroom intruder.

"No!" Isabella shouted, stepping in front of Sand, her hand up and outstretched, fingers splayed in a "Stop!" gesture, protecting her new business partner—and, more importantly, the million on the bed.

Some women had a maternal instinct, but Isabella Silva had a materialistic instinct, which did not serve her well when in that crucial fraction of a second she came between John Sand and her lover's bullet.

As Isabella slipped to the floor, her eyes wide with a concern not at all monetary now, hand on her belly with red squeezing through her fingers like cherry jam, Sand yanked the silenced .45 from his waistband and squeezed off a round.

The general took it in the shoulder, right under the epaulets. The impact and pain sent his revolver tumbling from fingers that popped open, and Barrios himself to his knees, clutching his right shoulder, then rolling onto his side.

Sand knelt by Isabella, who lay in a sexless sprawl on a puddle of pink satin. She raised her head and whispered something through bubbling blood, something he barely heard.

But he heard it, all right, storing it away for later use.

Her head lolled back. She seemed to be staring over Sand's shoulder; he glanced back, and up, at her smiling full-figure form in the gilt-frame, so triumphantly towering over her tiny country, her gown the color of the blood that no longer bubbled.

Shouts filled the hallways, footsteps clomping in their direction. Sand went to Barrios, who was clutching his shoulder with his own cherry jam to worry about, half-propped on his side, wide tortured eyes wet to overflowing.

Sand took the general by his good arm and hauled him to his feet, garnering an anguished yelp.

"They're coming," Sand said softly. "Get rid of them."

"*Vete al infierno,* gringo!"

Go to hell.

"I will hold you hostage and walk you to Silva," Sand said. "Your soldiers will come along with us and see and hear it all."

Fists banged on the door. *"General! General Barrios!"*

Sand said, "They knew right where to find you, didn't they? I talked to Silva last night."

"You *couldn't* have!"

"Scaled the wall and strolled right in. He knows everything you and the late First Lady have been up to. He'll talk and I'll walk."

"General!...Break it down."

"Get rid of them," Sand said.

"*Todo esta bien!*" the general yelled. *"Mi arma se disparó accidentalmente!"*

His gun had gone off accidentally, he told them.

Probably not the first time in this suite, Sand thought.

"*Está seguro, general?*"

"*Estoy seguro! Déjanos! La Primera Dama y yo tenemos mucho que discutir.*"

Barrios and the First Lady, it seemed, had much to discuss.

And then the voices ceased and the footsteps receded.

Sand collected the general's pistol while the man sat on the floor, trembling, probably going into shock.

The secret agent went to the door, cracked it, checking for any soldiers who'd been left on guard or just to keep an eye on things. Apparently none had been. Perhaps they knew not to linger outside the First Lady's quarters when the general's voice from within told them to go.

Sand asked, "Can you walk, General?"

"Too weak..."

"Give it a try."

Sand hauled him rudely to his feet, and drunk-walked the groggy general down the hall to the makeshift hospital room of *el Presidente* Silva, taking the briefcase along.

They went in unannounced, Sand shutting the door behind him, the general stumbling, shoulder bloody, eyes bleary.

Silva sat up in bed. "Señor Sand! Explain yourself."

After depositing the general in a chair, as if dumping a pile of kindling, Sand quickly filled Silva in—that he'd killed the assassin targeting Silva but that Stacey Sand had been kidnapped. That he'd confronted Isabella, who had been shot and killed by Barrios with a bullet intended for Sand.

"Is he dying?" Silva asked, his eyes wide taking in the weeping, wailing general. No concern or interest was expressed about his late wife.

"Not yet," Sand said. "That will be up to you, sir, unless he won't tell me where my wife is being held. Then I'll be a one-man firing squad."

Silva got out of bed, yanking the taped IV off his hand,

the needle already detached. His pajamas were sweat-stained and rumpled, but he had renewed vigor. He padded over barefoot.

"What do we do, Senor Sand?"

"Do you trust your soldiers?"

"I do. All but the general here."

The general leaned back in his chair, whimpering, clutching his shoulder, the uniform sleeve damp with blood.

"I can summon them," Silva said. "I will tell them you are a national hero, because that is the truth!"

"That's appreciated but premature. I brought you something." He went over and put the briefcase on the hospital bed, *el Presidente* following. "That's a cool million, literally. Oil testing rights for Boldt. Acceptable?"

"Of course! You'll want it in writing."

"A handshake will do for now."

They shook hands, Silva's still bearing some IV tape, and yet surprisingly firm. Amazing what one night away from heavy sedation could do for a man.

Sand said, "What I need is some time with the general here."

Silva gestured with the open hand of a gracious host. "Be my guest."

"The general and Isabella and the assassin they hired engineered my wife's kidnapping, and Barrios here is the only person living who knows where she's being held, save for the son of a bitch who has her."

Silva shrugged. "Do what you must to get the answer. I will watch. I might enjoy it."

"You may not," Sand said. "Would you agree to any offer I might make him?"

"I owe you whatever you ask—except for the contents

of that briefcase. I have my people to answer to."

"No, that money is yours. And San Ignacio's. May I?"

"Please."

Sand went to the seated, sobbing general. He lifted the man's chin with a forefinger and locked eyes.

"General, I don't believe in torture. Sometimes it works, sometimes it doesn't. Just not dependable intel. And I can't threaten the life of the woman you love, because *you've* already killed her."

The general's groan seemed to start at his toes.

"Tell me where Ernest has Stacey," Sand said, "and I will give you your life."

"My...life?" Silva's moaning stopped; his discomfort had likely *not* stopped, but Sand certainly had his attention.

"Your miserable life, yes."

To Silva, the disloyal general asked, "Would you do this? Honor such a pact?"

"You would be banished from San Ignacio," Silva said, "put on a plane to some agreed-upon destination."

"And I will ask Presidente Silva," Sand said, "to allow you to hold onto any wealth you've accumulated. To liquidate any belongings before you leave your homeland. I frankly wouldn't care if you stayed, but I can't ask the leader of your country to have such an appalling traitor in his midst.... *Well?* Where do they have her?"

Barrios was in shock now; he looked close to passing out.

But he managed, "The very last cottage at the back the of the compound."

CHAPTER SIXTEEN
SAND TRAP

That Ernest might be waiting for him, with plenty of support, Sand knew was a genuine possibility. With Leonardo on his swim to nowhere in the guest cottage pool, and the assassin's driver dead and dumped inside, no one was around to check in with Ernest, and assure him that Sand had been safely either (a) dispatched, or (b) sent packing.

Added to that was the possibility that someone on the Isabella/Barrios payroll may well have reported the presence of a very much alive John Sand at the palace this afternoon.

The element of surprise, in mounting Stacey's rescue, might well be gone.

That is, unless Sand could come up with a surprise Ernest hadn't contemplated.

Barrios had told Sand that four guards would be stationed outside the cottage. Despite army uniforms, these would be hard-bitten mercenaries in Leonardo's employ. Presidente Silva had offered any back-up Sand might feel necessary, but Sand said thank you, no, fearing possible turncoats within the ranks. The late Leonardo's driver, after all, had worn the uniform of the San Ignacian army.

By occupying the last cottage against the rear wall at the west end of the palace compound, Ernest likely figured that should Leonardo's plans go wrong in any way—as they of course had—Sand would be compelled to launch a direct assault.

As he drove the black Lincoln through the front gate, turning south, Sand felt certain that Leonardo's arrogant acolyte would be confident that even the storied Sand would never attempt to scale a ten-foot-tall stone wall topped with shards of broken glass. So what other option *was* there but a frontal attack?

At the end of the compound, Sand swung west. The probable assumption that the wall was an insurmountable obstacle provided Sand with the perfect weakness to exploit. Turning north, he slowly cruised the west wall from outside the compound, finding the street of hotels and government buildings quiet, with modest traffic and no sign of soldiers or suspicious vehicles indicating security measures on the late Leonardo's part.

Sand parked on the grass with the Lincoln's passenger door almost flush with the compound's wall, ten or perhaps fifteen meters beyond where he calculated the cottage would be. Still behind the wheel, he leaned over to collect the floor mat from the rider's side. After pocketing the keys, he exited the vehicle, taking along the black mat.

This late in the afternoon, Ernest might anticipate Sand waiting until nightfall to make his move—the cottages occupied a section of the compound rather under-illuminated after dark, after all. Had the hostage been anyone but the former Stacey Boldt, that might have been a reasonable assumption. But John Sand wasn't about to postpone his wife's rescue for a second longer than necessary.

He climbed onto the boot of the Lincoln, then up to the limo's roof. The heat and humidity of this goddamned country would just not let up, and his suit coat didn't help; but he needed it for the extra ammo magazines it held and the half-size combat knife. As for Leonardo's .45, even if Sand removed the noise suppressor, the thing was bulky and prone to jamming. Hell with it. The Walther could do his talking. And the knife.

He reached up and, quietly as he could, draped the floor mat sideways over wall's upper ledge, and its teeth of broken glass.

Hoisting himself atop the floor mat, chest, then belly, he could feel the glass teeth poking him, but thankfully not making it through the heavy fabric. He pulled himself around, legs hanging, with a view on the cottage and its shallow back yard. The structure was a little to his left, so he had estimated its position fairly well. Below, a meter-wide border of underbrush hugged the wall.

From here he could see only one guard, in a soldier's uniform with a rifle on its strap slung over his shoulder, a sidearm on his hip; at parade rest, the rather stocky guard was positioned next to the cottage, facing away from Sand—evidence, if any were needed, that Ernest anticipated a frontal attack.

Sand was slightly concerned that the layout of the place might be different from where he and Stacey had been staying. He had assumed all the cottages were the same, but the pool was off the kitchen at the rear of theirs, while this backyard was just a grassy patch. No pool at all perhaps?

Nothing to be done about it now.

Sand leapt, landing like a cat, if a cat wore rubber-sole shoes, just past the underbrush border and onto a manicured lawn. Crouching, he unbuttoned his suit coat for easy access to the Walther, then filled his hand with the combat knife from the coat's left-hand pocket.

Staying low, he crept up behind the guard until he was right behind him. Only when Sand rose from his crouch was the sentry at all alerted, but not in time to do anything about the hand clamped over his mouth or the knife blade that cut his throat, spraying the lawn red before him.

Sand wiped his blade on the trousers of the dead guard, who was face down in the short, bloody grass. Then, crouching again, he quickly followed a waist-high hedge row along the rear wall of the cottage. When he peeked around the far corner, at the left side of the little bungalow, he confirmed that the place was indeed somewhat differently laid out than theirs. The pool and its patio were tucked in here, accessed by a screen door that indicated the kitchen was not directly behind the living room.

A more immediate problem was a second guard, seated at the small metal table near the pool, legs crossed, his rifle on the table. He was smoking, lounging, a young, skinny guy in his twenties, dogging his duty. A dozen feet separated Sand from the guard, with no cover between them, no way to sneak up on him.

Actually there was a way, just not an ideal one.

Sand slipped into the hedge row hugging the cottage and got down low between the wall and the roots of the hedge, like a groundhog looking for shade. He crawled like a groundhog, too, just not as quickly or as nimbly. If he were heard, he'd be just a big dead animal shot to die in the bushes.

So the going was slow. The only aural cover came from the pool making little lapping waves, thanks to a breeze the ocean had decided to share. Sand could see the guy sitting there, smoking, as he and his combat knife got closer, closer. At some point he would be close enough to just jump out and...

The guard stood, his metal chair screeching, dropping his cigarette, grinding it out with a boot toe, suddenly vigilant.

In the low bushes, where he thought he'd been making little noise at all, Sand froze—*what the hell had he done to alert this lazy bastard?*

A second, older, far more seasoned-looking guard was approaching the kid, now on his feet. Relief flooding him, though he remained frozen, Sand realized *he* hadn't spooked the guard—this other sentry had.

The older guard cursed out the younger man in Spanish, utilizing language Sand, who was fairly conversant in the tongue, did not always know. San Ignacian dialect, perhaps.

After working up a sweat chewing the young guard out, the crusty mentor wandered out of the inset area and back toward his post in front, shaking his head in disgust at this younger generation. Suitably chastised, the once lazy guard now looked alert and ready. Then Sand came out of the hedge, clamped hand over mouth and cut the kid's throat, spraying the pool with arterial blood that recalled an earlier encounter in the day.

Having had enough of crawling around in the bushes, Sand stepped around the corpse of a youth now grown as old as anyone ever got. Then he ran around to where, near the front corner of the cottage, the self-righteous guard stood with wide-planted feet as he used binoculars, likely trying to spot Sand making that fabled frontal approach; hearing someone coming hard and fast, the sentry turned to face a man barreling at him headlong to jam a combat knife in his belly and, with a practiced twist, empty the sentry's entrails onto the grass while a rough hand covered his mouth and his wide eyes looked into the face of the very man he'd been looking for, then those eyes—no longer wide—filmed over, and he fell.

A final guard, Castro-bearded and husky, came around from the front, fast, but only had time to mutter, "*Mierda*," before Sand flung the knife expertly and sent it deep into the guard's chest with a *thunk*, as if amplifying the last beat of the man's ruptured heart.

Sand had taken out all four guards, without making much noise at all; without knowledge of the layout of the cottage, however, he said to hell with it and came around to the front and went in.

Stacey was on a rattan couch, on her back, her knees up, still in the Yves Saint Laurent jumpsuit, ankles bound, wrists bound before her, a gag around her like a misplaced headband. A pillow for her head had been thoughtfully provided. Her dark, mascara-smeared eyes were huge, her eyebrows high, as she saw her husband come in with the Walther in hand.

Standing next to her was Ernest, in his impeccable livery, sans cap however; that affable, helpful black chauffeur.

"Put the gun down, Mr. Sand," Ernest said, ever polite. "I have no desire to kill your pretty wife, but I will. I will."

"But you won't," Sand said, and shot him in the right eye.

And so ended the tour guide to end all tour guides, who tottered, the gun falling from dead fingers with a *clunk* to the hardwood floor, a moment before their owner flopped backward with a furniture-rattling *whump*.

Sand ungagged his bride, kissed her quickly hello, untied her hands, then her ankles. She was saying, "Did you risk my life just now?"

"I would have been a wealthy man, if he'd got a last shot off. Don't you know that?"

She was beaming. "You are such a terrible man."

"They teach you *anything* in school? A head shot shuts off all motor skills."

A car pulled up noisily outside and, within seconds, a shockingly fit-looking Jose Silva entered. He wore a spotless, perfectly pressed white suit—the picture of a Caribbean despot, or an ice cream salesman.

"We've been keeping an eye on you, Mr. Sand," *el Presidente* said. "From a respectful distance, of course. And this is your lovely wife!"

Stacey, her ankles free, got to her feet, shaky but typically spunky. "Rumors of your illness appear to have been exaggerated."

"Yes." The leader of San Ignacio glanced at the nearby corpse of the dead chauffeur, who was staring at the ceiling with two dead eyes, each ghastly in its own way. "If you will allow me to escort you gentle people elsewhere, we can talk in rather more comfort."

Stacey gestured to her somewhat rumpled designer togs. "I would like to freshen up, if that's all right, Your Excellency. Might we stop at our own cottage for a few moments?"

"I'm afraid," he said, "your husband has left it in a rather untidy condition. I've arranged for a suite in the San Ignacio Hilton for your use, for the rest of your stay. Your things will be transferred there. If that will be acceptable."

"Oh," Stacey said brightly, "John stays at the Hilton on all his Caribbean trips."

***

Their hotel suite, amusingly, was not unlike what Sand's *Habana Libre* might have been like, in Batista days. There they indeed freshened, and perhaps more, but not until he had filled her in on his rather busy day since they'd last seen other, from the two encounters with Isabella and the death of Leonardo, to trading Barrios his life for her whereabouts and the assault on the hostage cottage. He left out only the gory details, perhaps afraid she might have enjoyed them.

Her tale was somewhat simpler—Ernest had picked her up in the limo, with a story about her husband having sent for her urgently, only to be chloroformed and, well, at least Ernest hadn't had his way with her. He'd been very polite, really, for a psychopath who always smiled too much when he told her he hoped he wouldn't have to kill her.

They dined in a private nook of the hotel restaurant, guests of *el Presidente* Silva, to whom Stacey, over her *arroz con gandules,* said, "We understand you do business with Anthony Morello."

Silva, dining on his stewed salt fish with dumplings, looked mildly alarmed. "I must admit that I do. You are people of honor and might rightly be offended by this. He is a *culebra*, no doubt...but his money helps the people of my country."

"You should know," she said, "that Fat Tony may claim that the briefcase John left with you came from him. In a way he would be right. But it was our payment, to prevent your...abrupt removal from office."

"Ah."

The waiter came with Dom Perignon. Silva deferred to Sand, who sampled the stuff and approved it.

"He may claim he has a share of our proceeds," Stacey was saying, "if our oil tests lead to a profitable partnership with San Ignacio. But he has no such rights. If you feel you must pay him something, we understand. But not from our share."

"Understood. You have my word."

Stacey smiled. "Just so long as you know he's a snake."

"Yes, Mrs. Sand. But you should know that I am a mongoose—a mongoose who intends to educate and feed his people."

After dinner, they had dessert and coffee.

"About the oil," Stacey said.

Silva shrugged. "You have the tools, I have the oil...or at least that's what we've both been led to believe."

"Yes," she said.

"If oil is found, if production begins, I will consider the briefcase an advance payment. But San Ignacio will require half of all net profits. That is what I want, and what my country deserves."

Stacey smiled and glanced at her husband. "Dear, do you think we did the right thing, saving this man's life?"

Sand shrugged, more interested in his Jerk chicken. "Too late now. He lives and breathes and sits before us."

Silva gestured and smiled. "Trujillo asked for a million or more merely to explore, did he not? And only then would you see profits."

Stacey raised her glass. "President Silva, perhaps it's the food, or the champagne...but I accept."

The trio toasted.

***

The next morning, flying home First Class, the Sands were served more champagne, if not Dom Perignon. Stacey held her husband's hand, like a schoolgirl with her beau, gazing at him in much that same way.

"John Sand," she said, "a night with you in the tropics

is like no other."

"It's a gift," he said.

She was studying him. "Is there something wrong?"

"No. No. It's just been..."

"The best of times, the worst of times?"

He gave her a little kiss. "Always the best with you, my dear."

But Sand was keeping something from her, which he knew was a breach of their bond. It was just that knowing what she might do, how she might react, frightened him worse than anything Leonardo might have visited upon him.

Should he share the last words of the First Lady of San Ignacio? Those terrible six words that Isabella had whispered to him?

"You will never stop Jake Lonestarr."

Could the man who murdered Stacey's father—who had tried to kill her—still be alive?

A LOOK AT LIVE FAST, SPY HARD (JOHN SAND BOOK TWO)

John Sand, the former MI6 agent upon whom a certain fictional spy was based, is keeping a secret from his new bride Stacey – he has been tracking the supposedly dead Jake Lonestarr, her Texas oil tycoon father's traitorous business partner.

When Stacey disappears, is Lonestarr responsible or Las Vegas godfather Anthony Morello – a man with a big grudge – or is it the shadowy figures behind the slaughter at the new international spy agency trying to recruit John Sand?

The search for the beautiful Mrs. Sand – who has her own deadly charms – crosses continents, as Sand navigates a death trap in Berlin, an attack in a neon graveyard, and an earthquake in Mexico, with an army of assassins everywhere he turns...leading to a most dangerous game in the jungles of Curacoa.

"John Sand wows in this exciting spy adventure!"

AVAILABLE NOW

MAX ALLAN COLLINS
RANKS THE JAMES BOND FILMS

I began reading the Fleming Bond novels in junior high, when I ran out of Mickey Spillane books. In fact, that's how James Bond was marketed by NAL, Spillane's own publisher—Fleming as the British Spillane, Bond as the British Hammer. In such early novels as *Casino Royale* and *Live and Let Die*, the influence is undeniable.

When the film DR. NO came out, I convinced my parents (on a school night) to drive me thirty miles to the nearest screening. I wanted to see it opening day. None of my classmates had any idea who Bond was. That would change. I consider the moment when Connery first uttered, "Bond, James Bond" as the most memorable one of my long and storied moviegoing experience.

I went on to read the new books as they came out (starting with *On Her Majesty's Secret Service*—in hardcover). By high school, Bond was a craze, and some young males even wore 007 after shave. You would have to tie me in a chair and beat me about the genitals to reveal whether I was one.

I will admit freely that I, like most of my friends, carried a briefcase to school, because of *From Russia With Love*. Several of us carried starter pistols in our briefcases. Today we'd go to reform school for that. Do they still have reform school?

The years passed, and I married my own Bond girl, Barbara Mull (not Bach—though Ringo and I are both lucky guys). In those pre-VCR days, Barb and I would sit through any new Bond film twice (starting, fittingly, with *You Only Live Twice*). The Bond films were frequently re-circulated as double features. I saw them again and again in movie theaters.

Barb, who many have noticed is very smart, has a slightly different view than mine regarding the individual Bond actors. She feels each was right for his decade, and that none of them (save for Connery) was likely to have worked in any other decade. That's a theory worth considering, even discussing.

However, those any of you with lesser credentials than mine as listed above need not criticize or argue with my listings. Keep in mind that you might be secretly sitting on an ejector seat right now.

RANKING THE BOND FILMS

1. GOLDFINGER—the gold standard. Great villain and hatchet man, strong women, wonderful score featuring Shirley Bassey's dizzying rendition of the Anthony Newley/Leslie Bricusse/John Barry title song. Best lines in any Bond film, particularly: "Do you want me to talk?" "No, Mr. Bond—I want you to die!" Heaven.

2. FROM RUSSIA WITH LOVE—faithful Fleming, with a Hitchcock feel. Best romance and best fight (with Robert Shaw in a train compartment). Lotte Lenya the greatest "henchman," and an effective introduction of uber-villain Blofeld (who was better before we actually saw him).

3. DR. NO—defining moment. Connery immediately inhabits the Bond role so thoroughly, fifty years later it's still his. Everything flows from the colorful template established here, and Bond's Mike Hammer-like ruthlessness changed action movies. "That's a Smith & Wesson, and you've had your six."

4. YOU ONLY LIVE TWICE—overblown fun. Roald Dahl—in for Richard Maibaum (who scripted or co-scripted 13 Bonds!)—seems to be putting Bond through the paces somewhat mechanically, but the setting and set-pieces (particularly the attack on the villain's lair) are stunning, the size of it all staggering. Most of *Austin Powers* flows from here.

5. THUNDERBALL—the series at its popular, Beatle-mania-esque peak, but self-parody (jet pack anyone?) is creeping in, and the underwater sequences are interminable. So-so villain in a dubbed Aldolfo Celi as Largo, but the women are fine (particularly cheerfully evil Luciana Paluzzi), and Connery's cool as Bond is at its pinnacle. Wonderfully over-the-top Tom Jones title song.

6. THE LIVING DAYLIGHTS—return to Fleming-style Bond. No one seems to like Timothy Dalton but me, but of course I'm correct in considering him the second-best Bond. The film is very much a *From Russia With Love-*

style spy film, with a convincing romance and incredible stunts. Dalton was able to return to Connery's ruthlessness while bringing a more human quality to the character. A pity there weren't a half dozen Dalton Bonds.

7. ON HER MAJESTY'S SECRET SERVICE—placeholder masterpiece. Lazenby might have grown in the role if the producers and directors had worked with him; instead, their contempt for the departing Connery was visited upon his replacement, who balked. Nonetheless, *OHMSS* rivals *From Russia With Love* in its Fleming faithfulness, and is a stunt-heavy, lavish production with some genuine emotional impact. Telly Savalas as Blofeld is hurt by his latter-day *Kojak* fame, but Diana Rigg offers a timeless, tender Tracy.

8. LICENSE TO KILL—more nasty Fleming-style Bond. In part an adaptation of Fleming's novel *Live and Let Die* (the alligator attack on Felix Leiter), *License* is a gritty crime/espionage caper with more great stunts and another strong Dalton performance. A genuinely menacing villain in Robert Davi, who bonds with Bond.

9. DIAMONDS ARE FOREVER—real Bond if not quite glittering. Connery is back, seeming a little out of place in the '70s, but still the genuine article; a fine John Barry score includes a Shirley Bassey title-song vocal. The film is occasionally Cubic Zirconia, however, leaning rather too hard on the Vegas setting, subjecting us to Jimmy Dean as a Howard Hughes type, with a shipboard villain's-lair attack sequence that is among the most boring. Good Blofeld in *Rocky Horror*'s Charles Gray, whose gay henchmen (Bruce Glover and Putter Smith) are memorable, and die "flaming."

10. CASINO ROYALE—gritty, satisfying reboot. Craig's self-confident, rather brutish arrogance overcomes what initially seems like miscasting in a surprisingly faithful updating of the first Fleming novel. A strong romance helps make this a "real" story, and mind-boggling stunts take the series up a notch. Craig is easily the best Bond after Connery and Dalton.

11. NEVER SAY NEVER AGAIN—the real Bond in a strong remake. Probably more entertaining than the film it reworks (*Thunderball*), *Never Say Never Again* presents a slightly tongue-in-cheek Connery having a better time than in his previous several Bond appearances. Wonderful Bond women (not girls) in Barbara Carrera and Kim Bassinger, and a better Largo in Klaus Maria Brandeur. HALL OF SHAME: lackluster Michel Legrand score. With a John Barry score (and the James Bond theme), this would be much more popular among fans. (A bootleg version of the film is scored with Barry music from other Bond films, and is much superior to the official release.)

12. THE WORLD IS NOT ENOUGH—Brosnan's best. A tricky plot reveals that Brosnan, like Dalton, has the capacity for both ruthlessness and genuine emotion. The film, which features an *I, the Jury*-esque showdown between Bond and a femme fatale, is usually dismissed because Denise Richards plays a nuclear scientist. Right—Bond films frequently have female roles and female casting choices that make a lot of sense....

13. GOLDENEYE—Brosnan makes a strong debut, splitting the Connery/Moore difference, a killer who can quip. A big, stunt-flung production, *Goldeneye* has several

memorable performances, including Sean Bean (prefiguring the rogue double-o agent in *Skyfall)*, Judi Dench as M, Famke Janssen as a femme fatale/henchman, and Alan Cumming as an irritating computer programmer, whose death is extremely satisfying.

14. TOMORROW NEVER DIES—Brosnan hitting his stride. Again, stunts take centerstage, in part because of the Hong Kong action influence represented by Michelle Yeoh, who is one of Bond's strongest female counterparts. The media mogul villain seems well cast in Jonathan Pryce but the result is surprisingly flat, as is an attempt at emotion by way of old flame, Teri Hatcher. This marks the first of David Arnold's wonderful Barry-esque scores.

15. SKYFALL—Daniel Craig hitting his stride. While it doesn't entirely cohere, director Sam Mendes' Bond film is visually stunning and always compelling, walking a fine line between nodding/winking at the 50th anniversary of Bond and dragging the franchise screaming and kicking into the 21st century. But Bond fails at everything he sets out to do in this one, which ultimately is odd.

16. QUANTUM OF SOLACE—underrated *Royale* sequel. The opening car chase is a mess, and a lot of the action sequences suffer from frenetic editing. But mostly this one gets an undeserved bad rap, though admittedly it works much better when watched a day or so after *Casino Royale*, as the Part Two it intends to be. Despite rumors that a writer's strike left the screenplay unfinished, the vengeance theme is well explored, probably better than the similar *For Your Eyes Only*. Craig is working out just fine.

17. THE SPY WHO LOVED ME—the best Roger Moore, hands down. Surprisingly, Moore is mostly not at fault for the campy, smirky nature of some of these films—he usually plays it straight, while the producers lay on the dumb humor. Here, in a return to bombastic *You Only Live Twice* lavish production values, with a strong romance by way of rival Russian agent Barbara Bach, Moore acquits himself respectably, as does the film, with a decent Dr. No clone of a villain in Curd Jurgens, and a superior villain's-liar attack sequence.

18. FOR YOUR EYES ONLY—the second-best Moore. The opening, in which an unnamed Blofeld is killed off, is offensively jokey, particularly considering that it begins with a reference to Bond's late wife, Tracy. But the rest of this vengeance-driven tale finds Moore playing straight with the plot actually mattering. And for once, the underwater stuff is effective, not snooze-worthy.

19. DIE ANOTHER DAY—Brosnan left stranded on the ice. And it's a pity, because the film begins well, with an outlandish action sequence that leads to Bond's imprisonment and a rogue-agent set-up that promises to be the best of the Brosnans. Not the case—the horrendous third act includes an invisible car and a poorly executed ice-surfing sequence (at least the producers didn't dub a Beach Boys song over it), and a villain who is about as threatening as a hall monitor. HALL OF SHAME: participation of Madonna, whose title song is almost as bad as her stiff cameo as an improbable fencing mistress.

20. LIVE AND LET DIE—terrific Saint movie. Too bad Roger Moore is supposed to be playing James Bond. Blax-

ploitation aspects have dated the film, but remain a part of its unique appeal. Jane Seymour makes a fetching Bond girl, the voodoo stuff is fun, and McCartney's title song is no-contest the best non-John Barry music in the series.

21. THE MAN WITH THE GOLDEN GUN—good villains, weak everything else. Christopher Lee as hitman Scaramanga and his little henchman Herve Villechaize are memorable to say the least, but the rest of the enterprise represents a tired retread of Moore's debut film. Britt Ekland makes a surprisingly irritating, ineffective Bond girl, and the chop-socky stuff isn't nearly as well-integrated as the similar material in *Tomorrow Never Dies*. HALL OF SHAME: return of hick Southern Sheriff J. W. Pepper (taking nothing away from Clifton James' classic portrayal of corrupt Lt. Quint on TV's *City of Angels*). An example of how the Bond producers pander to audiences.

22. A VIEW TO A KILL—slightly underrated if over-long Moore finale. Christopher Walken makes a nicely menacing, psychotic villain, and his "henchman" Grace Jones is similarly memorable. Tanya Roberts (one of numerous Bond girls who are also Mike Hammer dolls) is fine in a role she's often criticized over—you were expecting maybe Meryl Streep? The film is surprisingly violent (Moore dislikes it for that reason). HALL OF SHAME: a Beach Boys song, "California Girls," plays over an otherwise straight ski chase...not even the real song, but a sound-alike cover version.

23. MOONRAKER—outer space nonsense, as the Bond producers keep pandering. A really wretched film, in which the previous entry's memorable evil henchman (Jaws) is

turned into a good-hearted comic relief character, and the villain is a buffoon with a ridiculous goal absurd even for a Moore film. Blatant product licensing. The pits. Well, almost the pits....

24. OCTOPUSSY—Bond as a literal clown. Worst villain in a puffy-looking, bored Louis Jourdan. Stiff acting from Maud Adams as the title character. The producers dub the "Tarzan" yell over an otherwise straight action sequence. The vault copy of this one should be cut up into guitar picks. This was released the same year as *Never Say Never Again* (the movies essentially tied at the box office) and demonstrated, as if anyone needed any further evidence, that Connery was Bond and Moore was the Saint. Or maybe Beau Maverick.

AUTHOR'S NOTE

This typically opinionated piece first appeared in 2012 as part of my weekly Update/Blog, at www.maxallancollins.com. Posted every Tuesday on the web and on Facebook, with essays, memoirs, news and occasional book giveaways.

ABOUT THE AUTHORS

MAX ALLAN COLLINS was named a Grand Master in 2017 by the Mystery Writers of America. He is a three-time winner of the Private zEye Writers of America "Shamus" award, receiving the PWA "Eye" for Life Achievement (2006) and their "Hammer" award for making a major contribution to the private eye genre with the Nathan Heller saga (2012).

His graphic novel Road to Perdition (1998) became the Academy Award-winning Tom Hanks film, followed by prose sequels and several graphic novels. His other comics credits include the syndicated strip "Dick Tracy"; "Batman"; and his own "Ms. Tree" and "Wild Dog."

His innovative Quarry novels were adapted as a 2016 TV series by Cinemax. His other suspense series include Eliot Ness, Krista Larson, Reeder and Rogers, and the "Disaster" novels. He has completed twelve "Mike Hammer" novels begun by the late Mickey Spillane; his audio novel, Mike Hammer: The Little Death with Stacy Keach, won a 2011 Audie.

For five years, he was sole licensing writer for TV's CSI: Crime Scene Investigation (and its spin-offs), writing best-selling novels, graphic novels, and video games. His tie-in books have appeared on the USA TODAY and New York Times bestseller lists, including Saving Private Ryan, Air Force One, and American Gangster.

Collins has written and directed four features and two documentaries, including the Lifetime movie "Mommy" (1996) and "Mike Hammer's Mickey Spillane" (1998); he scripted "The Expert," a 1995 HBO World Premiere and "The Last Lullaby" (2009) from his novel The Last Quarry. His Edgar-nominated play "Eliot Ness: An Untouchable Life" (2004) became a PBS special, and he has co-authored (with A. Brad Schwartz) two non-fiction books on Ness, Scarface and the Untouchable (2018) and Eliot Ness and the Mad Butcher (2020).

Collins and his wife, writer Barbara Collins, live in Iowa; as "Barbara Allan," they have collaborated on sixteen novels, including the "Trash 'n' Treasures" mysteries, Antiques Flee Market (2008) winning the Romantic Times Best Humorous Mystery Novel award of 2009. Their son Nathan has translated numerous novels into English from Japanese, as well as video games and manga.

MATTHEW V. CLEMENS is a writer and teacher whose first book was a non-fiction true crime title, Dead Water: the Klindt Affair (1995, with Pat Gipple). He has co-written numerous books with Max Allan Collins, the pair having collaborated on over thirty novels and numerous short stories, as well as the much-lauded non-fiction work, The History of Mystery (2001). They also contributed an essay to the Edgar-nominated In Pursuit of Spenser (2012).

In addition the duo has produced several comic books, four graphic novels, a computer game, and over a dozen mystery jigsaw puzzles for such famous TV properties as

CSI (and its spin-offs), NCIS, Buffy the Vampire Slayer, Hellboy, and The Mentalist, as well as tie-in novels for Bones, Dark Angel and Criminal Minds. A number of the team's books made the USA TODAY bestseller list.

Matt also worked with Max on the bestselling "Reeder and Rogers" debut thriller, Supreme Justice (2014), and shared byline on its two sequels, Fate of the Union (2015) and Executive Order (2017). He has published a number of solo short stories and worked on numerous book projects with other authors, both non-fiction and fiction, including R. Karl Largent on several of the late author's bestselling techno-thrillers. He has also worked as a book doctor for numerous other authors.

Matt lives in Davenport, Iowa with his wife, Pam, a retired teacher.

Made in the USA
Columbia, SC
25 April 2021